Blythe Court

Blythe Court

BY

Vicki Hopkins

ROMANCE WITH A KISS OF
SUSPENSE

RED BRICK MEDIA

DEDICATION

In honor of my second great grandmother, Ann Seddon. Born 1829 in Little Hulton, Lancashire, United Kingdom; Died 1898 Lancashire, United Kingdom.

ONE

MY PRESENTATION

My skirt billowed around my body as I sat upon my sore tailbone in the middle of the parlor. "This is impossible," I screamed, pounding my fists on the floor. On the verge of expelling an unladylike curse, I pulled myself up into a standing position and heaved a sigh.

"Now dearest," Mother cajoled, "I have confidence that you can master the technique before your presentation."

"I sincerely doubt it," I said, flinging back a loose strand of hair dangling in front of my nose. "I have absolutely no sense of balance."

"Once again," Mother instructed, wiggling her finger at me to carry on. "Extend your right foot behind your left."

Determined to succeed this time, I moved into position. My hands clutched the fabric of my dress on both sides, and I closed my eyes to focus upon the task without distraction.

"Back straight, Ann. You are slouching."

"Yes, Mother." I pulled my shoulders into alignment and bowed my head to the floral-patterned carpet beneath my feet. The ball of my right foot balanced behind my left one, resting level and straight upon the floor. Mother continued giving directions.

"Slowly lower your body downward, bending your knees. When they almost touch the floor, remain—"

"Bloody hell!" A curse spewed out of my mouth as I lost equilibrium and tumbled hard onto my already bruised bottom. The fall jolted me so severely that tears welled in my eyes. My fifteen-year-old brother burst into hysterical laughter, watching me from the threshold of the parlor double doors.

"Make sure you don't yell 'bloody hell' in front of the Queen, sis, or you will never marry." Ralph held his stomach while he roared a hearty laugh. "Ann is going to be an old maid, old maid," he bellowed, taunting my failures.

"Good gracious, Ann Seddon," Mother gasped. "Such uncivilized vulgarity!" My mother glowered at me in disdain with a scrunched brow of displeasure. Embarrassed over my curse, my cheeks grew warm as they burst crimson red. Little did she know, I had a terrible habit of cursing under my breath.

"Forgive me," I said. My voice trembled. "I am frustrated and tired. May we stop for the day? My presentation before Queen Victoria is not for another week." My hand wiped my sweaty brow.

"At the rate you are going, you will never be ready," Ralph snickered. "You're a clumsy girl."

"Oh you," I growled, fed up with his teasing. A plump pillow resting on the divan caught my eye, and I decided to fling it at the rascal. It flew through the air with ease, heading straight for his head. He ducked just in time to escape the wallop. In horror, I watched it soar through the doorway and hit my father in the face. He stood rigid after the jolt, and I cringed at the scolding that would momentarily ensue.

"What in the world is going on here?" he bellowed. Father wobbled his head a few times, shaking off the effects of the blow. He bent over and picked up the pillow from the floor.

"Oh, Father," I implored, running toward him. "I am so sorry. Forgive me." I glared at my brother, incriminating him in the act. "The pillow was meant for Ralph. He's been teasing me and calling me an old maid." Father cleared his throat and handed me the projectile.

"I came to investigate what the ruckus was all about," he said.

"Ann cannot complete the full curtsy," Mother replied. She walked forward and jerked the pillow from my hands, giving me another disapproving glare over my childish behavior.

"Hey, I innocently stood by," Ralph interjected. "Can't a brother watch?"

"You scoundrel," I replied. "Stop teasing me and laughing at my failures."

"Ralph, do as your sister bids," Father's commanding voice boomed. "Leave her in peace."

"Yes, sir." Ralph lowered his head in defeat and shuffled down the hallway.

"Well, I will leave you and your Mother to continue with your lessons." My father narrowed his eyes, and a small smile curled the corner of his mouth. "As good as you are at flinging a pillow across the room, I am confident you can perform a simple curtsy."

"Thank you for your assurance, Father." I

was pleasantly surprised to witness a hint of humor emerge from my austere parent. He had been keen on marrying me off as soon as possible, which undoubtedly served as the motive behind his encouragement. He glanced at Mother and back toward me and nodded, then turned and left the room.

"All right, one more time," Mother demanded.

"I would rather go to my room and practice alone," I replied. With lips pressed together in a hard line, I boldly postured my preference. "Perhaps I shall master it without your wiggling finger and Ralph's laughter at my failed attempts."

Mother cocked her head to the right, pondering my suggestion. "You might have a point there, my dear."

She stepped forward and expressed a sympathetic grin. At first, I thought she might embrace me to offer comfort, but she kept her distance. Unrestrained displays of affection toward family members were forbidden at Hartford Court. My father, an earl in the county of Hampshire, thought it a despicable practice to display emotions while in common areas. Behind closed doors and out of the ears and eyes of servants were the only exception. However, even then, my parents lacked the ability to embrace their children. It saddened me that my governess Miss Peel would soon depart my care upon my eighteenth birthday. She had been my sole source of affectionate display.

"All right, I will excuse you to practice in your room. My only request is that you advise me when you overcome your lack of balance. You know that I worry about what Her Majesty will think of you."

Of course, Mother worried what everyone thought of the Seddon's, from the most impoverished tenant on our land to the Queen herself.

"I promise to keep you informed of my progress," I assured her.

"Perhaps Aunt Adeline will help," she added as an afterthought.

The dowager duchess and sister of my father would be my sponsor during the presentation. Due to arrive in a few days, our household would be overrun by her extravagant entourage. Aunt Adeline was a stickler for all things aristocratic, whether it be manners, speech, or how one dressed and carried themselves.

"Well, I hope to have mastered it by then,"

I announced. The very thought of Auntie giving me instructions sent shivers down my spine. I loved her because she was my aunt. However, it didn't mean that I necessarily enjoyed her company. I thought her to be the perfect example of aristocratic snobbery. Her regard for the lower class bordered on contempt, while I never possessed such attitudes. People were people and deserved respect and kindness, regardless of their status in the scheme of societal rank.

Not wishing to discuss the matter further, I pulled up the hem of my skirt and swirled around, heading for the doorway. I had no problem whatsoever with my skills in balance when it came to escaping Mother's expectations.

While sprinting up the staircase, I pondered the dreadful fact that soon my parents would begin their pursuit of the perfect mate for me. Any possible male suitor would be exposed to their excessive scrutiny, and I pitied what they would endure. At least my involvement would be minimal as my only obligation would be to display myself as an engaging and desirable young lady.

The undeniable fact remained—my parents would choose my husband. Even though the practice of arranged marriages had lessened compared to decades past, my parents refused the contemporary thought that I should be permitted to marry for love.

At last, I had conquered the difficult curtsy only a few days before the ceremony and became confident that I would do well. Mother and Aunt Adeline insisted on watching me beforehand to make sure that every inch of my royal bow was correctly executed. After receiving accolades of approval, the next few days were spent ensuring that my dress appeared flawless in every aspect.

The garment, especially procured by the best seamstress in the county, looked absolutely stunning upon my slender frame. The long train, on the other hand, proved to be a challenge. My aunt insisted that I practice how to handle the yards of material flowing behind me. She took a long tablecloth and pinned it to the back of my day dress for another practice session.

"You must move gracefully, Ann, and glide across the floor," she admonished. For hours, I glided like a bird in flight, not flinching to the right or left.

Having mastered the walk, the momentous day arrived. I looked ravishing in my white dress and flowing train, with a tulle headdress and feathers. As the carriage halted in front of St. James's Palace, I observed a line of beautiful young ladies with their sponsors enter through the doorway. I knew beforehand exactly what to expect since my aunt had taken me step-by-step through the entire procedure.

We exited the carriage, and I carefully folded my long train over my left arm. Aunt Adeline stood next to me with her face aglow with pride. My parents, of course, were bursting with excited anticipation as they watched our movement forward.

Carefully, I stepped into the palace and glanced at my surroundings. We had entered into a long gallery that led to the Presence-Chamber where I would wait until properly announced. My parents would remain behind with others who watched their daughters with pride.

"You already know what to expect," my aunt reminded me.

"Yes, I have it memorized completely," I

assured her. The evening before, I even dreamed about the honorable event.

A few moments later, we halted before double doors. A few other young ladies were in line before me, waiting to enter the Presence-Chamber. As instructed by my aunt, I lowered my train. The Lords-in-waiting hastily spread it carefully behind me, preparing me for my steps forward. A card with my name inscribed upon it had been handed to another Lord-in-waiting. A moment later, he succinctly and loudly announced my arrival to the Queen of England.

"Lady Ann Seddon of Hampshire."

Suddenly, my heart fluttered, and I feared that I would faint. Inhaling a deep breath, I approached Her Majesty, nervously clinging to a small bouquet of white baby roses and carnations. At that moment, a pivotal point in my life had arrived that I had fantasized about as a little girl.

After gliding across the carpeted path as instructed by Auntie, I stood before the Queen and began my curtsy. With all the grace I could amass after hours of practice, I flawlessly lowered myself before the Sovereign in humility. With my head bowed,

I could not discern her facial expression as she gazed upon my presentation. As a daughter of a peer, her Majesty kissed me on the forehead instead of me kissing her hand. The overwhelming moment passed before me like a fantasy, and I rose to an upright position after a victorious display. I had all but forgotten my aunt standing nearby who witnessed the formality.

My introduction signified that the Queen approved of my admission into society as a suitable young lady worthy of being courted. Truth be told, I found the act of bowing before the monarch more exciting than the prospects of marriage that loomed before me.

After standing erect, I genuflected to the other members of the royal family. Another name was announced, and I backed out of the room gracefully without tripping over my train. As we exited, my aunt lauded me with congratulatory remarks.

"Stellar presentation, dearest. I am very proud of you." She eyed me approvingly. "You are the most beautiful of young ladies here today."

"Thank you, Aunt," I said, finally taking in a deep breath to calm my jitters. Each second sped by so quickly that I barely took note of the Queen's appearance. Saddened at how swiftly the moment passed, I wished that I could have taken a more extended look at the royal family.

We returned to the large gallery where other families waited for the return of their daughters. Upon seeing my approach, my parents smiled warmly at me. My father appeared proud as a peacock.

"Well, did all your practice pay off?" he inquired.

"Yes, Father, I did not fall," I answered, gathering my train back up on my left arm once again. The dress was dreadfully heavy with its numerous yards of fabric. I planned to keep it until my dying day as a memento of my accomplishment.

"I'm so very proud of you, my dear," Mother added. "Now, it's time to find you a husband."

Mother's rapid switch from approval to resolve did not surprise me one bit. I rolled my eyes and braced myself for the impending quest. Tonight I would attend my first ball and probably meet potential suitors.

Two

The Search

After the regal and lavish debutante ritual, the social season began. Parents throughout England could not wait to introduce their available daughters to eligible bachelors in want of a wife.

Like any other young woman of wealth and aristocratic blood, I had been painstakingly bred to be the spouse of a distinguished man of title. My mother told me, in no uncertain terms, to put aside the idea of romance before marriage. Nuptials of convenience were to blend family fortunes and keep pedigrees intact. My parents would negotiate my matrimonial contract with another family as if I were a horse to be sold and used for breeding.

As a young lady, I accepted my lot in life and did not often entertain the thought of amorousness. Nonetheless, I did have preconceived ideas of what I would and would not tolerate in a marriage relationship. Even though I had been told not to expect too much from wedlock, I hoped to secure an amicable bond with a benevolent man. If I found an ounce of happiness, as my mother put it, I would be grateful.

Mother did not hesitate to warn me about the challenges of marriage. Early on, she encouraged me to seek other avenues of entertainment should I suffer from a lack of attention. Pursuits such as shopping for the latest fashions, traveling abroad, taking the waters at Bath, and social events were always agreeable activities. Besides, I enjoyed the out-of-doors and pursuits such as horsemanship, a rousing game of croquet, and competitive archery matches. Honestly, I held no fear of being able to amuse myself while my husband went about doing whatever it is that husbands do to run their private affairs.

My primary responsibility in marriage, of course, would be to produce an heir for my husband to continue his lineage. By some means, I hoped to curtail the number of children I would be expected to bear, dreading the thought of continually being pregnant year after year. As long as a few young boys were brought into the world, my matrimonial duty would be complete, and a line ensured. Unfortunately, perishing in childbirth would always be a possibility, but I intentionally refused to dwell on such an unwelcome outcome.

After my presentation, and with those goals in mind, I entered into a whirlwind of tea parties with prospective mothers-in-law. My parents wasted no time in presenting my qualifications to respectable and influential families. Grand balls and other activities filled my calendar while searching for the right man to wed. Mother whispered tantalizing names of prospects into my ear, announcing how many pounds a year they were worth and what title they would inherit upon the death of their father. My parents assured me that I deserved the finest match my dowry could provide.

All the same, rather than being excited about the prospect of becoming a wife and future mother, I found the introductions tiresome after the first month. My mother wrung her hands with worry that I might pass the season without a proposal. Nevertheless, my father had many connections within society and evidently had his eyes upon a few prospective beaus long before my coming out. He had spent a significant amount of time carefully studying ancestral lines of various families in Burke's Peerage, narrowing down the possibilities.

As we sat together for afternoon tea, contemplating my current state of affairs, Mother expelled her discouragement.

"I cannot believe that we have not found a suitable bachelor," she sighed. Her brow furrowed, sadly gazing at me as if I were doomed to be a spinster.

Even though my younger brother's voice haunted my thoughts with his taunting words of "old maid," I attempted to keep positive. Perhaps there were more ladies on the market than men this season, but there still remained plenty of time for an introduction.

"You need not worry, Mother," I assured her with a warm smile. "I shall not cry myself to sleep should it take another season to find a husband."

"Another season?" Mother's eyes widened

in horror.

Over dramatic in her response, I concluded that my mother exaggerated the situation.

"I have confidence the problem is all but solved," Father said, interrupting our moment together by entering the parlor.

"Have you found someone?" Mother rose to her feet in eagerness.

"Perhaps," he said, glancing over at me with a reassuring smile. "Lord Bellingham and I chatted over a glass of brandy and a good cigar at the gentlemen's club this afternoon." Father paused for a moment, trying to suppress a sly smile. "Naturally, I mentioned that you were experiencing your first season, and he mentioned that the Duke of Dorset would be attending the ball this evening."

"A duke, you say?" Mother briskly queried, brightening in countenance as if she had been resurrected from the grave.

"Yes. Apparently, his son has been encouraged to take a wife."

"Is he the firstborn?" Mother inquired with excitement.

"Mother," I said in a scolding tone. "What does it matter if he is first, second, or third?"

Her questions were irksome and expectations far from reality.

"It matters, my dear, if he is to assume the dukedom upon his father's death," she spouted. "I don't wish you to marry a struggling secondary son who must earn his fortune."

"Yes, he is," Father replied, giving my mother a cautionary look to calm down. "At present, he has taken the duke's secondary title of the Marquess of Dorchester."

"Excellent!" shrieked Mother, clapping her hands together.

My father turned toward me and announced another tantalizing detail. "I hear he is one of the most sought after bachelors this season. After reviewing his lineage, I can say that it is rather impressive."

"Well, this could be the one," Mother confidently announced.

"Don't you think I should meet him first before we jump to conclusions?" I asked. Mother ignored my comment and continued to badger Father for more information.

"What is his name?"

"John Broadhurst," he replied. "Lord Bellingham remarked that the ladies appear enamored over his handsome appearance."

"He probably has a wart on the end of his nose," I remarked morosely.

"Ann," Mother retorted, keenly displeased with my comment.

"Don't you think it would be preferable if you allowed me to search on my own and let fate take its course?" I asked, holding my hands as if I prayed. The search by my parents had excluded me completely, giving me no voice in the matter.

"Absolutely not," Father swiftly replied. The brow above his right eye arched, accenting a pleased twinkle in his eyes. "I have a distinct feeling that this young man may be the one."

"And how can you be so sure?" I pressed for an explanation. "I've not yet made his acquaintance. It's quite plausible, Father, that the man will find no interest in me whatsoever."

"I can assure you, Ann, that will not be the case. As providence would have it, the Duke of Dorset arrived at the club and joined us for a drink. We had a rather interesting conversation."

"You did?" Mother's mouth gaped open as

she took a step closer to Father.

"I can only say that after an extensive exchange regarding our available offspring, the duke agreed his son would meet you this evening. In fact, he acted rather encouraged by the impending introduction."

"Splendid." Mother smiled approvingly and barked her next order. "Come along. We have much to do." Mother stepped toward the parlor door. "Now, Ann."

"Now?"

"If you are to meet him this evening, we only have a few hours to prepare you."

"We need not depart for another four hours," I reminded her, hoping to calm her down.

"Appease your mother's need to pamper you," Father encouraged me. "She has your best interest at heart."

Of course, Father was right. If I didn't succumb to Mother's insistence in transforming me into a desirable creature, we would all be victims of her cantankerous attitude, should it all come to naught.

"Coming," I replied with feigned eagerness.

"I'm ecstatic," Mother announced, entering my bedchamber. "You could very well be a duchess one day. How absolutely wonderful."

"You do realize, Mother," I began sternly, "that your expectations to succeed in attracting this young man places a burden upon me."

"Whatever do you mean, Ann?" she asked, not understanding my comment. "You have nothing to worry about. The marriage will be arranged and is out of your hands. It's not the young man's duty to approve of you. Rather, it's the duke's decision whether he feels you are worthy of his son. The same is true of the marquess. Father and I will make the decision if we find him acceptable." Mother smiled warmly at me. "You merely need to present yourself as the beautiful bred lady that you are, and I'm sure the young man will acquiesce with pleasure to the arrangement."

Her comment solidified the truth that I had no say in the matter. It did frustrate me to a point, but no recourse existed for me. Sighing in resignation, I perused my various garments and chose my newest evening gown of gold silk. The dress had been one of many purchased for the season, and Mother agreed with my choice due to its modest neckline.

In the hours that followed, my mother's personal attendant helped to arrange my hair into a stunning coiffeur, adorned with a jeweled comb. After a few dabs of modest makeup and perfume between my breasts, I put on the dress and transformed into an elegant creature. Mother entered my room, holding a necklace in her hand. I recognized the diamond from her overflowing collection of jewels that father had purchased for her throughout the years.

"Here, wear this," she said, coming behind me. The gold necklace and teardrop diamond draped down upon my bare neckline. My hand touched the stone.

"Oh, Mother," I gushed in appreciation. "Thank you."

"Now, young lady, remember to display your ladylike qualities with a singular purpose and decorum," she firmly instructed as she came to stand in front of me. "I'm very proud to call you my daughter, Ann."

My mother's accolades were not expressed often, and my eyes welled with tears. "Of course, I shall be on my best behavior," I assured her.

As we descended the staircase together, I saw Father below, grinning at me approvingly. We climbed inside the waiting carriage, and I wrestled with the enormous pressure to meet my parents' expectations. Tonight I could very well meet my future husband, and I struggled with fluttering butterflies in my stomach the entire trip.

Upon our arrival and entrance into the grand ballroom, my parents eagerly scanned the landscape of attendees for the Duke of Dorset. My father's keen eye caught sight of him at the other end of the room.

"There he is," he said, heading in the direction of the duke.

Mother and I followed behind along the sidelines. Couples waltzed to the current musical selection. Women swirled by and I could feel a breeze as the voluminous skirts of their dresses swirled around their ankles.

As we drew closer, I saw a man about my father's age watch as we approached. The duke eyed me curiously, then nodded toward my father and expressed a reserved grin. A woman stood by his side, and by her bearing, I knew it must be the duchess. A young man had his back toward us as we neared, speaking to another gentleman.

"It is a pleasure to see you again," the duke said, greeting my father warmly.

As soon as he spoke, his son slowly turned around. My breath hitched in my throat from excitement. I could barely breathe, waiting for the reveal. The tip of his nose bore no wart, and I stifled a chuckle at my earlier comment. Instead, his appearance bordered on near perfection. Every feature of his face lined in picture-perfect symmetry, accented by his glistening brown hair. I estimated his height a few inches above six feet in his well-tailored, silk waistcoat, but he had yet to look in my direction.

Flabbergasted, I sucked in a much-needed breath of air, thankful for his pleasing, good looks. I glanced at his mother and father, who were assessing my qualities or lack thereof at the same time. Suddenly, my father burst into a flurry of introductions. As I stood staring at the duke's son, I heard the exchange of formal titles between parents. Mesmerized and lost in girlish adoration, the duke's voice brought me back to reality.

"Lady Seddon, may I introduce you to our son, the Marquess of Dorchester."

At that moment, his eyes shifted in my direction. As he silently considered my presence, I continued to inspect his attributes. His piercing gray eyes, spotted with gold flecks, reminded me of a polished sword. He stood rigid, displaying no outward delight over the introduction. Instead of meeting my knight in shining armor, I stood before a sentry, warning me not to intrude upon the territory of his heart.

A surge of disappointment flushed through my body. Any enthusiasm I entertained at first glance of him instantly evaporated because of his cold and aloof gaze. I glanced at my parents as if they were ridiculous to recommend him as a potential husband. Perhaps I should have swooned like the other ladies nearby who watched our dull interaction. Even though he appeared like a dashing prince, he lacked the essential charm needed to make a good first impression.

After our awkward introduction, my disenchantment made it impossible to utter any good-natured remarks in return. I merely smiled demurely, attempting to draw out a reaction from his apathetic demeanor.

"Lady Seddon, it is indeed a pleasure to

meet your acquaintance," he began, bowing at the waist and extending his gloved hand. "Would you do me the honor of dancing with me this evening?"

Both sets of our parents watched as our first interaction occurred. I knew they expected me to accept, but I hesitated for a few moments, considering his offer. When my gaze shifted to his eyes, his brow creased in worry as if I might turn him down. Had I chosen to spurn him, I would never hear the end of it from my parents.

"Yes, I would be pleased," I replied, hiding my real sentiments. I placed my hand on his gloved palm, and the marquess gently led me to the ballroom floor.

He remained silent as he slipped his hand around my waist. We twirled around, dancing to a Viennese waltz, in a room filled with potential husbands and wives. His skills were impressive, and I kept up with his lead. As the music played, I waited for him to start a conversation, but he said nothing. When I glanced at his face, he showed no outward interest in me whatsoever. I thought him rude, so I prodded him to speak.

"You appear restrained," I said. "Is your

mind elsewhere?"

His eyes shifted in my direction. "I apologize, Lady Seddon. You are correct that I am distracted by other matters."

Handsome yes, but he sorely lacked personal appeal. "Then why did you ask me to dance if you were not interested in being in my company?" I put forward in a wounded tone. In reality, I felt angry at his slight attention as if my desirability merited more than he cared to give me.

"No doubt for the same reason you accepted my invitation to dance," he solemnly replied. "Our families have expectations."

His answer pricked like a thorn. It was cruel and cold, insinuating that I did not deserve anything beyond his unpleasant obligation to perform for his parents. I, on the other, had at least put forth a semblance of effort.

"Well, you should be commended, Lord Broadhurst, for fulfilling your duty," I snidely snapped. My demureness retreated due to my exasperated mood. Had my mother heard the tone of my voice, she would have surely slapped my face.

The music ended, and we swiftly released

one another. The marquess dropped his arms to his sides and took a step back to put distance between us as if I were a leper. His outrageously handsome face did nothing to sway my opinion of his poor manners. To my vexation, my rapidly beating heart betrayed my sensual attraction to him, nonetheless.

"Please excuse me," I said, swinging around and heading for the door to the veranda. The room had grown unbearably stuffy, and I needed to inhale a breath of fresh air. When I burst through the doors and walked out onto the patio, a cool breeze touched my flushed cheeks. A second later, I closed my eyes and inhaled a lungful to calm my irritation as my body trembled from the insult.

"How utterly infuriating," I grumbled beneath my breath. "He is ill-bred, without manners, self-absorbed, and. . . and. . . " My voice trailed off when I realized that my mother had come to my side.

"Why are you out here, Ann? You should be back in the dance hall with Lord Broadhurst."

My mother's hand grabbed my forearm. By the tight squeeze of my flesh, I sensed her displeasure.

"He acted like a conceited bore," I announced. "The entire time he spun me around the floor, his mind wandered elsewhere. He paid no attention to me whatsoever. When I reminded him that he held me in his arms, he barely came alive."

"Perhaps he was nervous," she replied, defending his actions. "You are, after all, an elegant young lady. Some men might feel intimidated in your presence."

I discarded her remark as inconsequential and was about to spew out my frustration when Lord Broadhurst walked out onto the veranda. He glanced about and caught my eyes, which I hurriedly averted elsewhere by turning my head in the other direction.

"It appears that he wishes to speak with me now," I informed my mother. "He is standing by the door."

Mother glimpsed at him and grinned approvingly. "Be forgiving," she said. "Our families have high expectations that this match will be advantageous." Naturally, she insisted on leaving another word of encouragement before returning indoors.

Lord Broadhurst slowly approached and

halted a few feet away. He bowed at the waist and viewed me with a hint of remorse on his face. To my shame, he still had the power to weaken my knees at one glance. I felt unworthy of any attention he might bestow when only moments ago I cursed him for giving me little if anything. His presence confused me.

"I believe I owe you an apology," he stated in a resolute tone. "My mind has been beset with matters that weigh heavily upon my heart. Regardless, it was unkind of me to allow them to interfere with our dance." He lowered his head, appearing like a child asking for mercy. "I humbly ask your forgiveness for my rude and insensitive behavior, Lady Seddon."

Somewhere amongst his gallant prose, I lost myself in his eyes and smooth tenor voice. His lips moved, and with each word, my heart pounded in response. I found it utterly impossible to remain ill-tempered toward him. By the time he had finished his apologetic recitation, I had already absolved him of any sin.

"We can all be prone to wandering minds at one time or another," I said demurely. My eyelashes batted wildly, acting helpless to stop my childish plea for attention. "I accept your apology and offer one for my abrupt departure."

The corner of his mouth tilted upward in a slight grin, but his eyes stayed dull and lifeless as if he did not mean a word of his expressed regret. Nevertheless, my mother's parting advice of forgiveness encouraged me to be a lady. I mimicked the tilt of his lips, determined to give him nothing more in return. We stood gazing at each other in silence, and I wondered what thoughts traveled beneath his thick hair.

"It appears, Lord Broadhurst," I said, being the braver of the two to start a conversation, "that our families desire us to become acquainted." He glanced sideways as if to avoid the topic.

"Yes, my father has indicated that our union would be beneficial." His inexpressive voice sounded as void of excitement as mine.

"The advice seems to be prolific amongst our parents, for I have been advised to turn my attention toward you."

I hated being the obedient daughter. His personality left much to be desired, but possibly my life would find some solace in gazing at his striking countenance until death parted us. My mind had wandered into a morbid pit.

"I might as well be forthright, Lord Broadhurst. I would much rather marry for love than blending family fortunes and giving you an heir." I postured myself like a snobbish imp. However, when I realized that I inferred intimacy and babies, my cheeks burned with shame. His brow over his right eye arched, and a flicker of amusement flashed across his face. Understandably, he found my brashness entertaining. "It appears that perhaps you hold the same sentiments," I added. His light-hearted smile faded as if I doused him with a bucket of cold water.

"Duty to my father and title are unalterable, Lady Seddon. I must do what is expected of me." He reached out his hand. "Would you allow me another dance? I will endeavor to place my best foot forward this time."

He held his gloved hand palm up, and I glanced into his eyes. While I considered whether to accept or not, a premonition of impending unhappiness swept over my soul. Conceivably not this evening, but one day he would shatter my heart. Of that, I was certain, and it frightened me. I glanced past his shoulder and saw my mother watching us from the doorway. I, too, had been expected to submit to my place in the scheme of society.

With trepidation, I placed my hand on his and watched his fingers wrap around mine. I surrendered to the unavoidable path of matrimony with a man I barely knew.

THREE

THE WEEKEND PARTY

Soon after the ball, we received an invitation to Blythe Court for a week-end house party. Since I finally had come of age to enjoy such festivities, I looked forward to the engagement for many reasons. The affair would comprise not only our family but also other prominent individuals from society who had single sons in want of a wife. I determined to keep my options open since I found the personality of the marquess guarded and aloof. Of course, I wondered who would be my competition amongst the guests of single ladies in quest of a mate.

Regrettably, like most country estates, the men would probably be off hunting during the day, leaving the women to fend for themselves. While they killed helpless fowl, foxes, and rabbits, the women of the household would drink tea, take strolls in the garden or gossip. Opportunities to mingle would occur with picnic lunches with the men, dinners, and entertainment in the evening.

Although Blythe Court was conveniently located about sixty minutes from our own residence, I had never heard of the estate. We traveled by carriage from our manor house in Hampshire to Dorset, the neighboring county. My parents were enamored with London society, and they rarely visited elsewhere. As we sat bouncing in our ride through the countryside, my curiosity piqued.

"Do you know anything in particular about the residence?" I asked my mother.

"It is an impressive estate," my father interrupted.

He always answered questions for my mother, which I found annoying. I often thought he had emotionally browbeaten Mother, in the same way he did to me now about my prospects for marriage. To my surprise, my mother shot him an annoyed glance and embellished his short report.

"The duchess told me that it was built in 1346, but modifications were made in the early seventeenth century. The south lawn faces a large pond, and the estate is circled by formal gardens." My mother grinned proudly over her knowledge of its history, which surpassed my father's curt declaration.

"It sounds quite impressive," I replied, snickering and using my father's description. Unfortunately, my flippant response received swift reprisal.

"I expect you, young lady, to spend the majority of your visit in the company of Lord Broadhurst," he spewed with authority. My mother joined the discourse.

"Under no circumstances are you to wander off unchaperoned," she warned. "At least not until he proposes, then in some circumstances you may do so with my permission."

My stomach balled into a knot. Any prospects beyond the man they already picked were clearly out of my reach.

"You speak as if you have already married me off," I protested. "Shall I not be allowed to talk with more congenial gentlemen in attendance?"

"Our solicitor is drawing up the marriage contract even now," my father brashly announced.

"What?" I wanted to lean forward, grab

him by the shoulders, and shake him like a rag doll. "Why on earth would you do such a thing without speaking to me about it or asking my opinion for that matter? I have merely shared a few dances with the boorish man."

My father's face turned beet red, and he opened his mouth to put me in my place. Thankfully, before the ill words were flung in my direction, Mother reached out and grabbed his forearm, stopping his gruff reply. In a civil tone, she spoke kindly to me but with firm conviction.

"Control your contentious attitude and act like the lady I bred you to be," she said. "You were told since you were a little girl that Father and I would arrange your marriage. Our wisdom in choosing you a good match should be all that you need to know."

"But—" My mother raised her hand halting my next words.

"We will speak of it no more," she declared. "One day you will be the Duchess of Dorset. Is that not enough for you?"

My mother's sharp words cut me off, and I leaned back into the seat surrendering rather than fighting. I glanced to my right, and my mouth opened in astonishment. We approached the front of the estate, and the horses trotted through a stone gateway onto a long pebbled path that led to the entry. An impressive three-story manor loomed before me. Like a curious child, I counted fifteen windows across the front facade and a massive arched doorway with columns on either side.

"My goodness," I said, gawking at the structure.

"My goodness, indeed," Father repeated. "The duke is giving Blythe Court to his son once he weds. This will be your home."

I sat motionless in utter shock over my father's revelation. Perhaps what lay ahead would not be as awful as I pictured in my mind. The most attractive man in the county and the most impressive estate imaginable were being given to me in return for obedience to my parent's wishes. A smile pulled my cheeks upward accenting my childlike dimples.

The carriage came to a halt, and a tall footman stepped forward, opened the door, and helped us out. The entire household staff lined up outside to greet our arrival. The duke and duchess appeared with warm smiles.

"It is good of you to come," the duke

remarked. "Ah, here comes another carriage," he said, looking past my father's shoulder. "It will be a steady stream of guests in the next hour."

I glanced at the doorway and saw John. He caught my eye and nodded but made no indication of pleasure upon seeing my arrival. Even in the bright sun, he appeared like a Greek god, and I cursed myself for being attracted to his appearance. He stepped forward and gave a quick bow.

"Lady Seddon, it is a pleasure to see you again."

"The pleasure is all mine," I replied with a curtsy.

He turned his attention to my father and mother, exchanging pleasantries, and afterward offered his arm to escort me indoors. Both of our parents grinned in the confidence of their success. When I touched him, it resurrected my previous impression of wariness over a potential union of our hearts.

We stepped through the doorway, and the entrance hall astonished my senses. Giant pilasters rose to a high ceiling, and medieval tapestries adorned the walls. John halted in the middle of the foyer, and I carefully surveyed the impressive interior.

"Mr. Rhodes, our head butler, will show you to your rooms," the duchess announced. "The footman will bring your luggage. It will afford you the opportunity to relax before our evening festivities."

John released my arm.

"I hope that you find your accommodations to your liking," he said. "I have requested that your room overlook the gardens and pond."

His voice sounded strained, and I concluded he found no pleasure in what had been arranged for either of us. My heart, full of disappointment again, withdrew into the shadows of my soul for protection. Perhaps spending time with him during the weekend would be more of a burden than a delight.

"Thank you," I responded. "I am sure that I shall be comfortable."

Mother nodded at me to follow her up the staircase, which I did without glancing back at my intended. A moment later, I found myself far too curious to see whether his eyes followed my departure, so I peeked over my shoulder. He had disappeared.

Dressed in one of my finest evening gowns, I sat at a large table filled with guests that arrived for the weekend. The dining room was located to the east of the entrance hall, a library to the south, and two impressive drawing rooms to the north.

A quick perusal of the table gave me the chance to examine any other single men in attendance. I soon learned that only two other gentlemen from prominent families arrived, but neither appealed to me. Understandably that would be my reaction since I had been ruined by the fetching male sitting to my left. He accidentally brushed his hand against mine as he picked up his fork.

"Excuse me," he said.

A flicker of kindness sparkled in his eyes, and I immediately snatched it as a keepsake in hopes of what lay ahead.

"Of course," I replied, making sure that I returned a demure and well-mannered response. Out of the corner of my eyes, I caught my mother's occasional glances. Father engrossed himself in a manly discussion with the duke while my mother chatted intermittently with the duchess.

"Are you acquainted with everyone at the table?" I asked John curious about the attendees at the weekend house party.

"Yes, I am acquainted with them all," he replied. "Shall I discreetly give you names between sips of my soup?"

My eyes sparkled at the idea of irreverent gossip between courses. "If you do not mind." He wasted no time in pointing out the guests.

"At the far end of the table sits Sir Riley of Yorkshire and his wife, Lady Elizabeth." He lowered his voice to a whisper. "You will discover that her laugh sounds like a snorting pig."

I had nearly choked on a spoonful of soup, but it would have been easy to do so after his irreverent disclosure. As he recited names, I found it impossible to keep my eyes off his face.

"Lady Seddon," he said. "Pay attention, for I will be testing your memory later."

Embarrassed, I ceased my gawking but discerned that he merely meant to jest rather than scold. As he spoke, I noted other females who apparently could not keep their eyes off John.

"Who is the young lady with the auburn hair and purple gown?" She occasionally glanced over at the two of us.

"That is my cousin Charlene," he replied. He paused and slightly lowered his voice. "She has her eyes set on Reginald Brighton, a mere accounting clerk in Dorchester. It is the family scandal, you see, and I fear she will elope and cause a stir."

After letting out a sigh of relief that she was not my competition, I replied. "I dare say she is a courageous young woman, but no doubt she will be a poor one if she marries beneath her position," I said. "Although I do not blame her for pursuing love." The way I vocalized my thoughts, they sounded snobbish. I immediately regretted my statement.

"Not only poor," John interjected, "but dead to the family. My uncle will not allow her to set foot in their home again if she disobeys his wishes."

"Do you think it fair?" I asked, eyeing him curiously to obtain his opinion.

"Fair has nothing to do with it," he said. "Whatever opinion I hold on the matter will be my own."

The tone of his curt reply told me that he

did not wish to share his thoughts, which I found unkind. I envisioned the steel sword pointed in my direction, so I dropped the subject entirely.

The footman served the next course, and I turned my attention toward my dinner plate to contemplate what lay ahead for the weekend. Since my father revealed that the marriage contract had been handed over to the solicitor to draft, I wondered if I should expect a proposal during the activities. Curious regarding the schedule, I began prodding him for information.

"Shall I expect the barking of hounds in the early morning hours to wake me up?" The hunt usually started at dawn with howling dogs and eager horses. Men in their tweed jackets, with dangling shotguns over their arms, would eagerly mount their saddled steeds and speed off into the countryside.

"I expect you will," he answered. "Most of the men come to enjoy a good fox hunt over the weekend."

"Poor fox," I sadly replied. "Frightened, chased, and outnumbered by yapping canines to be shot dead."

"I take it you do not approve." John

sounded displeased about my comment. "Do you mean to tell me that a beautiful lady like yourself does not own a fox fur?"

"Well, if you put it that way, I insist you hunt to your heart's desire. I shall not give up my winter coat with its fox collar that I find most comforting and warm." By now, he must think me a hypocrite.

"Spoken like a genuine lady of class," John smirked, appearing amused over my selfish pursuits.

Our dinner dissolved into a superficial conversation, which offered me little else to learn about his character. I conversed with others sitting nearby, making the most of my attempt to present myself as a lady with manners and dignity.

When the meal ended, the women at the table stood in unison and departed for tea. The men stayed behind for cigars and drinks. I did not give John any parting words or glance as I left. His guarded demeanor exhausted me, and I doubted that we would have a worthwhile personal conversation the entire weekend.

We entered the large sitting room down the hall, strikingly adorned in Elizabethan décor. There were twelve women in the group. John's mother, the duchess, quickly came to my side. My mother followed closely behind, and I noticed that Charlene lingered nearby. The family members appeared intent on learning more about me, which I found to be natural under the circumstances.

Though I conversed briefly with the duchess at the ball, we did not have the opportunity for an in-depth conversation about any particular subject. She motioned for me to sit next to her on the settee. I obliged and then waited for her to start the conversation.

"I do hope you are enjoying yourself, Ann. We are delighted to have you as our guest this weekend."

The sincerity in her voice touched me, and I responded likewise. "Thank you, your grace, I am quite happy to be here."

"You may discover that my son is a man of few words. He grew up quite shy as a young lad, but does his best to overcome the disability as a man."

"Shy?" Astonished at her explanation, I shrugged it off as an excuse for his behavior. Of course, I wouldn't dare disagree with the duchess, so I thanked her for the information.

"Yes, he has been rather guarded with me, but I'm sure that will change as we become more acquainted with one another."

We exchanged words on a few other non-essential topics until the other ladies caught her attention. The duchess drifted away to speak with them, and Charlene sat down next to me.

"I am Charlene Broadhurst," she announced without smiling.

"John mentioned you were his cousin," I replied. "It is a pleasure to meet you."

"Are you enjoying your stay thus far?"

"For the most part, yes," I replied. "Hopefully, the weekend will become more stimulating."

"Oh, I am sure it will. Give the men another hour, and they will fill the room to play a silly game of charades."

"Really?"

"Yes, and then watch the interaction between Sir Riley and Lady Whittemore," she said in a low tone. "They are having an affair."

The tidbit of scandalous chatter perked my ears. Even though it was not proper behavior to partake in the sin of gossip, I enjoyed juicy secrets.

"Oh, dear," I replied. "Does everyone know?"

Charlene coyly grinned. "Of course they do. Why do you think we have weekend parties? It is to mingle so unhappily married couples can partake in a tryst here and there. As long as it is discreetly done, no one really minds."

The smile on my face faded. Would that also be my future—a husband committing adultery? I glanced at my mother, who appeared engrossed in shameful chatter and suddenly wondered whether my father strayed from their marriage bed. If he had, did she know? My pleasant evening turned sour at the thought, and Charlene apparently realized its effects.

"I apologize, Lady Seddon, for speaking of such indelicate matters. It is thoughtless of me in light of your relationship with John."

"What relationship?" I curtly responded. "He has barely paid an ounce of attention to me since we met."

"It is difficult for John to do so," Charlene replied.

"Why?" I scowled.

"I dare not say anything further," her

voice quavered. "Already, I have said far too much."

To my surprise, she stood to her feet and wandered over to another group of ladies, leaving me behind to consider her words. As I glanced around the room, which would one day be my home, I decided that I did not care for the atmosphere. The lovely décor somehow turned disagreeable in my eyes. Mother meandered over and sat next to me.

"Mingle dear," she encouraged me with a pat on my arm. "Do not sit here like a wallflower."

I wanted to ask her about Father but decided that it was not the time or place to do so. It would be safer to remain ignorant about such hurtful affairs than dealing with the disappointment that my father strayed.

"Yes, of course," I said, rising to my feet. I joined John's mother again and a group of other ladies. The usual superficial chitchat ensued about fashions, hairstyles, and the weather.

The door opened, and the men arrived smelling of cigars and brandy. All the ladies perked up like wilted flowers watered by their presence. The atmosphere erupted with animated males and women who wanted to play games. I glanced at John, who wandered over to my side and sat down next to me on the settee. His arrival suggested duty and not want, but I restrained my disenchantment.

"Will you join in a game of charades?" I asked.

"Not my favorite game, I'm afraid. I prefer cards." His glib reply showed no favoritism in either entertainment.

"And what about you, Lady Seddon? Do you enjoy charades?" he asked, looking pointedly at me for a reply.

The marquess already played a game of make-believe with me from the moment we met. Shaking my head negatively, I spoke.

"Not really, but I'll join the game if asked. After all, life is filled with charades, isn't it?" I stated in a matter-of-fact tone with a smirk.

"I suppose it is." He grinned in return.

For a brief moment, we sat staring at each other. He appeared to be assessing my appearance. I, on the other hand, pondered his guarded personality. Something about John Broadhurst was not all that it seemed to be. The steel sword I sensed at our first meeting remained pointed in my direction. Apparently, he planned to guard his heart at all cost.

The impression caused me to wonder if someone had been there before me who perhaps wounded his emotions. If that were the case, obviously he had not healed, or a hardened scar had formed over the wound. Whatever the state of the center of John's soul, he wanted me nowhere near it. He guarded the entrance, like a sentinel. Because of it, I determined to tread lightly in the days ahead, wishing to be wounded no more either. My thoughts were interrupted by the duchess.

"Time for charades, ladies and lords," she chuckled.

"Shall we?" I asked John, standing to my feet and holding out my hand. "I'm sure we can manage the game."

"Why not," he replied, shaking his head as if he clearly understood my meaning. He took my hand, and we walked toward the eager participants for an evening of group theatrics.

FOUR

OFF TO THE HUNT

Below my bedroom window, hounds of all shapes and sizes barked loudly waking me out of a sound sleep. Curious to see the group of men and their horses, I grabbed a robe and put it on before looking through the pane. John stopped directly underneath, no doubt for my benefit. He glanced up, and when he saw me peering at the scene, he tipped his hat and winked at me. Naturally, his actions shocked me, and I wondered if I were dreaming. A few minutes later, they rode off following yelping dogs, and John disappeared into the woods. He did look quite dashing in his tweed jacket and top hat.

A soft knock came at my door. When I answered, I found a young woman clothed in a black dress trimmed with white lace on her collar and cuffs.

"Yes?" I said, wondering what she wanted.

"My name is Miss Melanie Wright, your ladyship. Please call me Melanie," she said, giving a quick curtsy. "Mrs. James, the house-keeper, asked me to serve as your lady's maid during your stay this weekend."

After deciding she posed no threat, I opened the door. Behind her, a housemaid stood, holding a tray with tea, slices of bread, and butter.

"I will be waking you each morning," she announced, "and Eliza, who is with me, will bring your morning refreshments."

"Well, that sounds more agreeable than barking dogs," I replied.

"Oh, yes, the hounds," she said with a giggle. Eliza set the tray down on my night table. "Shall I bring hot water to fill your tub, my lady?" She glanced at me anxiously.

The idea of lounging in a warm bath sounded relaxing. "Yes, if it is not too much trouble." Why I felt the need to say that I had no idea. I frankly enjoyed being pampered by a maid all to myself. I shared my mother's attendant, but with her constant demands, the woman barely had time for me.

"No trouble at all," she replied.

Melanie stood in front of me with her hands clasped together, looking at me inquisitively. She appeared younger than most lady's maids and had a pleasing appearance. Her lovely golden-brown hair accented her glowing complexion. When she spoke, her voice sounded soft and gracious. I found her presence most agreeable.

"After you bathe, I'll help you get dressed, my lady. The duchess likes to gather for morning prayers in the chapel at nine o'clock, and you are welcome to attend."

Morning prayers? I wanted to roll my eyes over that bit of information. I wondered if Lady Whittemore would be confessing her sins after spending the night in Sir Riley's bed.

"Perhaps," I responded reluctantly.

"Very well," she said, giving a quick curtsy.

The young lady disappeared through the door, and I nibbled my bread and drank tea. A full day of activity stretched before me. While the men hunted, the women would be strolling the gardens and then join them later for a picnic lunch. A smile spread across my face as I recalled the wink from John. Had it been a genuine action or merely for show? Only time together in each other's presence would answer that question.

After a long walk to the top of a hill, we found the men lounging in the grass. The servants had arrived beforehand, setting out baskets of food, blankets, wooden folding chairs, and serving chilled champagne. I had never seen such an extravagant outdoor picnic in my entire life.

The day turned warm and sunny, and I chose a yellow day dress and a large brim hat to keep the sun from burning my nose. The long morning stroll exhausted me, although when I saw John I perked up and smiled. He immediately came to my side, glancing approvingly at my attire and bonnet. I held his sudden interest suspicious but welcomed the attention.

"So, your lordship, did you procure my next fox collar?" I gave him an impish smile. He shook his head no.

"Your father shot one, but alas it looks as if I may come home empty-handed."

"What a shame," I replied. The marquess appeared disappointed over his failure to succeed in the manly pursuit.

John quickly glanced at his father, who gave him an encouraging nod. Afterward, he took me by the hand and led me over to a blanket that we claimed together. A footman brought us a basket to share. I checked its contents while John poured us a glass of wine.

"We appear to have cheese, bread, and various cuts of meats to dine on," I said, laying some items before us. Even though I relaxed in his presence, I couldn't help but wonder what John sensed being together.

"Do you feel pressured by your parents?" I suddenly asked. A part of me wanted to see if his change in performance happened for my benefit or to please others.

"I could ask the same question of you," he replied.

He leaned back on his elbow and nibbled on cheese. His long legs and lean body were so attractive that I wanted to throw myself at him. Thankfully, my parents had not chosen a bald and overweight man as my future husband. Perchance this arranged marriage had been a blessing in disguise.

"Somewhat," I replied, shoving chicken in my mouth, annoyed that he merely answered my question with a question. After swallowing, I asked again. "So what about you?"

He lowered his eyes and fingered a piece of bread. "Pressured is maybe not the right word to describe my emotions." Rather than finishing the thought, he nibbled on his food instead.

"There are times that I wonder if you feel anything, your lordship." My voice sounded annoyed, but I could not help expressing my growing frustration.

"You can be assured, Lady Seddon, that I do indeed possess passions about many things."

"Just not about me," I murmured in an undertone. Uncertain if John heard my comment or not, I turned my eyes toward the landscape, allowing the various hues of green to soothe my doubts. "You know," I said, not looking at him, "you do not have to go ahead with this arrangement. Surely, there are other choices."

I really wanted other options. A part of me wanted to fall violently in love and be swept off my feet. It would be exciting to be his passionate pursuit. By now, though, I had resigned myself to a mundane relationship, and a life filled with babies. Perchance I would chase illicit dalliances to fill the void like other ladies did, but inwardly I confessed that I didn't possess the nerve to sin for pleasure.

"My title and duty have their demands," he solemnly replied, "and I am prepared to concede to our parents' wishes." He reached out and touched my hand tenderly. "I am sure that we will grow to enjoy each other's company as time passes. Of that, I have no doubt."

His touch warmed my hand. Whatever ill feelings that I harbored over his poor attitude vanished. I wanted more than to enjoy his company for the rest of my life. Surely marriage had to offer something beyond companionship and bearing heirs. What about love? What about passion?

I lifted my eyes and looked at him warily. "Very honorable," I said. "Here we are. The picture of two obedient offsprings, willing to give up everything for the sake of money, title, and position. A pure union of convenience." When I acknowledged the fact aloud, it sounded absolutely dreadful to my ears.

A moment later, I stood to my feet and brushed off the crumbs from my skirt.

"Would you care to walk with me?"

"If you wish," he said.

After rising, he offered his arm, which I gladly took. A gust of wind pushed up the brim of my hat, and I grabbed it before it flew off like a kite. I did not wish to glance at my parents nor John's. We started to stroll, and I became curious about my beautiful surroundings.

"How many acres?" I asked.

"Thirteen hundred," he replied.

"What is that odd looking building over there?" I pointed toward a square tower on top of a nearby hill.

"It is a hunting tower, and we call it the cage," he replied.

"May I see inside?"

"Yes, of course, but shouldn't you ask permission from your parents to depart from the picnic?"

"No. Let us be scandalous and run off." I grabbed him by the hand and pulled him forward. He voiced no protest and followed along. I dared not turn around to see the gasps of my mother and father. We were clearly in their sight. Surely, they would not worry as long as they could see John behaving himself.

I trusted him implicitly not to take advantage of the situation. After all, he had not shown an ounce of interest to tempt me otherwise.

When we approached the structure, I stood there surveying the stonework. "So what is a hunting tower?" I asked. Frankly, I had no idea. Did the men go to the roof to shoot deer passing by the cage, as they called it?

"Its original purpose was a lodge for hunters when built in 1580. The park keeper used it for a cottage for many years, but it is empty now."

"Can we go inside and climb to the top?" I tilted my head and looked at the three-story structure. It would surely afford a prime view of the vast acreage of the estate. John glanced back toward the party guests, looking for any parental objections.

"Of course. I see no harm in it," he said.

He opened the entrance and led me inside the dark building. The window shutters were closed, but light illuminated the room from the open door. It took a few seconds for my eyes to adjust, and my nose wrinkled from the dusty and mildewed smell. A narrow staircase led to the second floor, and I followed John to the third. He flung open a door, and we exited to the rooftop. The bright sunlight caused me to squint, readjusting my gaze. I walked over to a waist-high stone perimeter and peered at the extensive estate.

"How beautiful." The scenery mesmerized me, bringing a reprieve from the awkward moment. It overlooked the moors and the acres of vast parkland that spread across the countryside. One day, all of this would belong to John, and if I married him, I would enjoy the beauty and solitude with our children.

John stood alongside. We remained silent. The leaves rustled in the trees nearby, and another windy gust flung my hat off my head. It took flight like a bird and whirled in the air.

"Oh my goodness," I shrieked. "It is quite blustery up here." I laughed while I watched my sunhat flip-flop across the green grass. At least it tumbled toward the picnic guests, and I hoped that Mother would grab it as it flew by.

My hairstyle fell apart around my shoulders. Strands whirled around my face in wild disarray. John reached out and gently brushed a lock of hair from my eyes. Uncomfortable by his touch, I lowered my head, wondering if he would do anything more. Would he dare to kiss me? I doubted he would before our engagement. Of course, I still had not received a proposal of marriage either, though we both knew that to be the ultimate goal.

Slowly I lifted my head. He looked terribly sad, and I wondered why. "Are you all right?"

"Yes, I am fine," he responded. John turned away from me. "We should return."

By the tone of his voice and grief-stricken countenance, he appeared miserable. My plan for a romantic moment vanished as if it too, had been carried away by the wind. I resigned my fate with a sigh and followed him down the stairs and out the door. We leisurely returned to the lawn party, and I saw that my mother had caught my hat, after all.

"Did you have a pleasant walk?" she asked, handing over my bonnet.

I flashed a feigned smile. "Yes, it was quite enjoyable." *No Mother, it was a complete disaster*, I grumbled to myself. After the failed attempt to bond with my intended, I wanted to return to Blythe Court and hide in my room. Maybe I would have an epiphany on how to win his heart.

FIVE

LOVELESS PROPOSAL

On Sunday evening, I prepared for our last dinner together. Melanie had been an excellent lady's maid, tending to my needs. She helped me dress and styled my hair. As I observed her pamper me, a part of me envied her simple life.

"When I return, will you still be here?" I had considered keeping her services as my attendant.

"You mean when you marry his lordship?"

"Oh, you know about that, do you?"

"Everyone does, my lady. It's the talk of the staff," she responded in a strained tone.

My brow rose. "I do not mind if you speak about it," I added. "It is merely an arrangement."

"We all think that you are fortunate to be marrying his lordship," she replied.

Melanie quietly finished my hair and helped to fasten a necklace. I rose from the vanity and grabbed my gloves.

"Well, then, I wish to thank you for helping me this weekend. If or when I do return permanently, I would like you to be my attendant. Would Mrs. James agree to such an arrangement?"

"If?" she repeated, looking curiously at me.

"Well, I have not received a proposal as of yet. The marquess hesitates to ask me, even though our parents have all but signed the contract."

"Oh, I see."

"If I do return as his wife, will you be so kind as to attend me?" I eagerly asked again, hoping that she would agree.

A broad smile spread across her face. "Oh, yes, my lady, I would be honored."

"It is settled then," I said. "You may go now, Melanie."

She curtsied and left me to assess my appearance in the mirror one more time. My attractiveness, I believed, pleased him. As far as my companionship, that was yet to be determined. If so inclined, this evening would be the time to propose. Perhaps he would decide to court me for a few more months. I despised not knowing what to expect in the hours ahead because it heightened my anxiety.

As I descended the stairs and joined the guests in the sitting room, my nerves prickled with apprehension. Most of the invitees arrived for drinks before dinner. John caught my eye and came over to my side.

"Lady Seddon," he said.

"Lord Broadhurst," I replied. My voice answered in the same glib tone as his own.

For a few quiet moments, he stared at me without speaking a word. I did the same in return, enjoying his attractive face and dark hair but not swooning over him like a silly schoolgirl any longer. Instead, I considered him like any other acquaintance. If he had shown me an ounce of affection the entire weekend, I might have acted differently. His lack of interest in me as a woman wounded my delicate ego.

"Have you enjoyed your stay at Blythe Court?" he asked.

Surprised he initiated the conversation, it took me a second to formulate my answer.

Should I tell him the truth about how I really felt? I decided upon a half-spoken falsehood if such a thing existed.

"For the most part," I replied, trying to restrain my negative sentiments.

Before anything further could be said, the room filled with the remaining guests, and we were ushered off to dinner. The usual seating arrangement continued, as well as the chatter around the table. Once again, John said very little of consequence until dinner ended. To my disbelief, when the women rose to retire to the sitting room, John did not stay for cigars and drinks with the men.

"Would you be so kind, Lady Seddon, as to accompany me for a short walk out-of-doors to the veranda?"

His invitation sent my heart fluttering, and I glanced at my parents, who nodded their head, granting permission. Surely, his actions meant an imminent proposal.

"Yes, of course, I would be delighted." My voice quavered, betraying my nerves. He offered his arm and escorted me to the terrace that overlooked the garden. There was a slight chill in the air, which added to the nervous goose pimples rising on my arms. Once outdoors, I glanced above to the heavens. It appeared the angels gave me a dreamy setting underneath the twinkling stars, but no romance swirled between us.

John halted his step. I sensed a trembling in his arm. It was endearing to think that he too struggled with apprehension. I found the courage to raise my eyes. He studied me as if he were reading a book line by line. His gaze wandered from the top of my head to the tip of my chin and rested on my lips.

"It is a lovely night," I said, trying to make light of the awkward moment. His silent pondering continued until he reached forward and took my hand. After giving it a slight squeeze, his lips parted.

"Lady Seddon, perhaps I should have made more of an effort to spend time with you this weekend," he began.

"Ann," I said. "Please, call me Ann."

A slight grin lifted the corner of his mouth. "Ann," he repeated.

My name sounded divine, coming from his voice. I sighed during the starry-eyed moment. "It has been a busy social affair," I replied, trying to make light of the short interludes we experienced together. "I'm sure we will have more time together in the days ahead." I prodded him toward the ultimate question and felt guilty for doing so. "That is," I clarified in a whisper, "if you wish to spend time with me."

He tightly squeezed my hand. My heart yearned to observe a spark of affection for me, but I only witnessed resignation. Suddenly, he was down on one knee.

"I desire to be with you," he said, sounding sincere. "And it is to this end that I humbly ask for your hand in marriage."

Finally, the most important time in my life had arrived. A man upon one knee, a proposal of marriage, but he spoke not one word of affection or endearment for me as a woman. He accepted our future together but failed to shower me with love. No doubt, his motives came from responsibilities—duty to his title, father, and fortune. He was bound in chains of obligation, and soon I would be bound as well.

For a full minute, I remained silent. I said nothing but searched John's eyes. As the seconds passed, he looked worried that I might refuse him. I knew if I did, my parents would disown me, and his parents would be displeased. Even if he did not reciprocate the little admiration that I held for him, he offered to be my husband. One day I would be a duchess and live at Blythe Court. Perhaps I would eventually win his heart, and we would experience love as husband and wife. As I considered the conundrum, I had no other course but to relent.

"I accept your generous proposal of marriage, Lord Broadhurst." With my hand, I pulled him from his knee until he stood before me. In response, he placed both of his hands upon my shoulders and stepped closer.

"Thank you," he whispered.

He lowered his head to kiss me, and I closed my eyes. I underestimated him completely. The kiss, sweet and soft, demonstrated a crumb of fondness for me. Thankfully, he acted with prudence, not prolonging the outward show of regard. If he had, I would have surely fallen from my weakened knees. At least John possessed the power to arouse my female longings. He drew back and held my hand in his.

"Perhaps we should go inside," he

suggested, "and announce the news to our parents."

He offered his arm, and we returned indoors. The men joined the women in the large parlor, and it appeared every eye scrutinized us as we entered. John walked toward his father and in a toneless voice announced my answer. "She has accepted." A broad smile spread across the duke's face as if a victory had been won and the spoils captured. I wondered how big of a dowry my father would hand over for my life.

"Ladies and gentlemen," his father quickly announced. "I would like to announce the engagement of my son the Marquess of Dorchester to Lady Seddon. Raise your glasses with me and let us toast to their happiness."

My blood rushed to my cheeks, and I blushed profusely. Every eye looked at the two of us, causing me embarrassment. John handed me a glass of champagne.

"To our happiness," he said. A warm smile curled his lips, which I had tasted only a few minutes ago.

"To our happiness," I replied. My eyes watered from emotion. Even though I would soon gain a husband, a grand estate, and a new life, a strange fear gnawed at me inwardly that one day he would shatter my heart.

I love the game of croquet. For some reason, I find it entertaining to whack a ball with a mallet. You get to direct the hard wooden object across the blades of grass, underneath wire rims, and finally to a tall post. At last, you hit it one more time, aiming at the stick in the ground. If you are lucky being the first person to wallop it to its destination and striking a pole, you have won the game.

After I accepted John's proposal, I swore I became that ball and everyone in my life the mallet. My existence had been swallowed up in a frenzy of preparations for the wedding. My mother enjoyed every moment pampering me, building my trousseau, and shopping until I wanted to collapse from physical and emotional exhaustion. She shoved me here and there and chattered at me unceasingly, fraying my nerves.

"Oh, Mother, we must rest! How many more things shall I cram into my trunk?"

"A young lady needs a full trousseau of everything imaginable in the way of under-garments, corsets, stockings, nightgowns, and whatever else we might find."

Had I known that preparing for a wedding would be so much work, I would have insisted we elope. I did not mean a word of it, of course. As the day approached, my excitement grew. John called upon me occasionally for short visits. It allowed us to deepen our relationship, but I still sensed that he did not love me.

I wanted to say the same of my heart, but after a while, he became impossible to resist. There were good qualities about his personality. His soft-spoken voice soothed my ears, and his appearance—well, I often felt mesmerized by his good looks and tailored clothes. John acted politely to a fault, always putting me first in my needs and tender when we touched. If marrying a kind man was a prerequisite to a healthy marriage, there might be hope for our union even if it lacked passion and love.

The wedding date had been set far too soon as far as I was concerned. The marriage banns, which were required to be read aloud on three Sundays before our ceremony, had been completed. No one objected to our union, of course, and everything proceeded on schedule. Next week I would walk down the aisle and begin my prearranged life. Of course, I possessed questions about what awaited me in the marriage bed. While my mother stuffed another pair of silk stockings into the trunk, I thought the moment would be a perfect time to ask.

"Mother," I began in a serious tone, "is there any wisdom you can offer before my wedding night?" She halted and looked at me wide-eyed. The frown on her face told me she found the subject indecent.

"You will find out soon enough," she quipped. "There is nothing you need to know."

Surely, there were things I needed to be aware of, and I determined to find out what they were. "Well, what should I do? How should I act when we are alone?"

My mother had done her Victorian duty in keeping me ignorant of the ways of men to protect me from becoming a fallen woman. My life had been so puritanically sheltered that my lack of knowledge brought me shame.

I did have my suspicions about what might occur but wondered if they were accurate. It became apparent to me that men were drawn to the sight of plump breasts, but the hidden treasures under my skirt were yet to be understood.

"Merely lay back, open your legs, and let him do what he does. If you find it bothersome, take your mind to somewhere more pleasant. Ponder the beauty of the English countryside; I usually do. Soon it will be over. They never take long to do the deed—at least your father does not."

"And will I get pregnant right away?" I thought it an apt question to ask.

"Well, that depends, dear, on timing and the Lord's will to give you children. I am sure, though, you will bear your husband a fine heir one day."

My mother continued to count my clothing and other items making sure I owned enough frivolous things to take with me. John had not told me where we were going on our honeymoon. Rather than sharing that task, he decided to keep it a well-kept secret. I hoped that it would be a pleasant place to offset any unpleasantries I might endure in the bedchamber.

"Well, it seems that you are intent on keeping me in the dark," I complained.

"The subject is not something proper ladies talk about," she quickly defended. "Now let us get back to the task at hand. We need to check with the seamstress today about your wedding dress."

My mother refused to enlighten me further. I had no one to ask either since I had been born the eldest in the family with younger brothers and a five-year-old sister. When the time came, I would experience the deed, and the mystery would be solved.

SIX

THE MARQUESS

Those dreaded words "until death you do part" resonated in my mind even after our vows were spoken. What had been done could never be undone in the eyes of God. I now belonged to John Broadhurst—mind, body, and soul. All of my worldly goods became his property. My individuality and single identity vanished, blowing away in a gust of wind, much like my hat did months ago. Whatever small amount of freedom I possessed as a young woman rose to the heavens and evaporated upon the pronouncement, "You are now husband and wife."

The same expression of duty and resignation remained in John's eyes, even at the altar. I, on the other hand, yearned for his affection. As our marriage was solemnized, I wanted his love. In fact, a deep ache rooted in my heart. We signed the marriage register and were presented to the congregation. A multitude of aristocratic guests filled Dorchester Abbey, and I braced myself for the congratulatory remarks that would soon ensue.

John smiled at me warmly, offered his arm, and led me down the aisle. I married the Marquess of Dorchester and the future Duke of Dorset in a grand ceremony. An exquisite wedding dress adorned my body, and I became the envy of every unmarried woman in the congregation.

The remainder of the day passed swiftly with celebrations. As the afternoon drew to a close, we prepared to leave for our honeymoon. Melanie met me in my chambers at Blythe Court to help me undress and redress for the journey ahead. When I entered the room, her demeanor surprised me. Tears welled in her eyes, which I found touching.

"Why are you crying?" I asked. She sniffled a few times and composed herself.

"Because I am exceedingly happy for you, my lady."

She drew near and looked at my dress with envy. I could not blame her because I realized her life would never be like mine. It was all right for her to wish for something equally exciting.

"Here, let me unfasten your tiara and veil, and we'll get you out of the wedding dress," she announced.

As Melanie began to release me from the multiple layers of lace, satin, and petticoats, I wondered if she had ever experienced love. My question was blunt and out of place, but nonetheless, it popped out of my mouth.

"Have you ever been in love?" My words apparently startled her because she ceased moving altogether. She inhaled a sharp breath.

"Yes," she meekly replied.

The smile on her face faded into obscurity. I intruded upon a private area of her life and regretted my inquiry.

"My question into your private affairs is clearly inappropriate. Forgive me." I lowered my eyes, ashamed to witness her distress. She remained silent in her duties, and I surmised that sometime in her life, a man must have broken her heart. My mind drifted to my own fears of John as if I braced for it to happen to me too. It was a terrible possibility to ponder on my wedding day, so I pushed it away.

A moment later, my dress was off and laid

upon my bed with care by Melanie. I changed into another day dress more appropriate for the trip ahead. "I see my trunk is gone. Have the footmen already loaded it on the carriage?"

"Yes, my lady. Everything has been taken care of as requested by your mother."

"I wish he would tell me where we are going." The tradition of keeping the honeymoon location a secret bordered on torture. My petty worries of having packed the right clothes for the trip plagued my mind. At least it took my cares to another place than the unknown wedding night.

"There now," Melanie said, assessing my appearance. "You look radiant." Her forlorn gaze persisted.

"Thank you for your help," I said. "I would take you with me, but John insists we travel alone without a valet and maid. Perhaps he thinks I won't need to get dressed for a week," I giggled. My unladylike comment apparently did not sit well with Melanie, and she lowered her eyes as if I had embarrassed her to death.

"I am sorry," I quickly added. "My nerves are making me far too chatty."

"Have a good time, my lady."

She curtsied and left. I proceeded downstairs to meet John. My heart thumped in my chest harder than it had during the ceremony. The anticipation of what would come in the hours ahead increased with each step.

He glanced up, smiled, and offered his hand. The entrance hall was filled with well-wishers, including our parents, who gave us departing hugs. My mother shed a few tears while my father gave an approving handshake to John. The duke and duchess wished us well, and my new husband swiftly spirited me off to the carriage.

After we climbed inside and the door closed, I glanced over at him. He stared out the window watching Blythe Court disappear as the horses trotted down the lane. Finally, he turned his attention to me. We were alone as husband and wife for the first time and beginning our voyage together as a married couple.

A few inches from my body sat a total stranger. I barely had become acquainted with him, except for his perfect manners. But who was he? What were his thoughts and aspirations? What were his passions in life or goals? What did he really think about me as his wife? I had absolutely no idea. My husband was an enigma. Hopefully, in the months ahead, I would discover the inner soul of John Broadhurst.

As far as our honeymoon was concerned, John decided upon a short four-week excursion, rather than an extended grand tour of one to three months. I had not traveled to the Continent before and hoped we would explore the world outside of England.

"Where are we going?" I prodded, hoping he would relent and tell me.

He reached over and held my hand. Even through his gloves, I recognized his cold fingers and realized how difficult the day had been for him too.

"Well, tonight we will lodge at a hotel in London. In the morning, we travel to Dover."

"Dover?" I repeated with excitement. "Are we going to the Continent?" My enthusiasm must have been contagious because John smiled over my animated question.

"I have decided," he said with a tone of mischievousness, "to make you wait until the morrow to tell you where we are headed."

"Oh, do not make me wait," I pleaded. "I will not sleep a wink tonight from anticipation."

"Oh, you will sleep," he replied, rubbing the back of my hand with his thumb. In slow circular motions, he stroked me thoughtfully. He had shown so little physical affection since our engagement, I wondered if he would now be more forthcoming in action. I hungered for him to embrace me, which he rarely did or even kiss me for that matter. John said nothing further, indicating to me that he refused to release his secret. Witnessing his tease gave me another small glimpse into his heart.

A rush of weariness flowed over me after a day of activity. My head tilted and leaned upon his shoulder. His body stiffened, but I refused to move. A few moments later, he slowly lifted his arm and put it around me.

"Tired?" he asked.

"Exhausted, anxious, nervous, afraid, apprehensive," I said. "Shall I go on?"

He looked down at me and brought his fingers to my chin. Gently he lifted my face until I looked into his eyes.

"You have nothing to fear from me, Ann."

His tone revealed sincerity, but I doubted.

Finally, the dreaded and uncertainty of our physical joining arrived. I took care of my toilette matters and let my waist-length locks cascade about my shoulders and back. After brushing out the tangles, it fell into wavy curls. My hair was my glory, and one of my finest features.

My mother had purchased a modest nightdress to cover me as if I were dressing for a winter storm. After putting it on, I glanced at myself in the mirror, encased in a cotton gown. It appeared entirely inappropriate. Puritanical or not, I was not my mother. I could not let John see me like this, or he would walk out and never consummate our marriage.

A second later, I pulled it up over my head and tore it off my body, throwing it in a heap on the floor. I stood stark naked in the middle of the room, glancing around looking for something to cover myself with before my husband entered. A soft knock came at the door. Panicked, I pulled the cover off the bed and wrapped myself in it like a cocoon.

"Come in," I squawked, swallowing a lump in my throat. I clutched the blanket tight. John entered, took one glance at me, and halted in his step. Actually, I made matters far worse. Instead of a nightgown, I covered myself entirely in a puffy blanket. My idiotic attempt to woo my husband into wanting me turned into a catastrophe. It looked as if I were wrapped in a downy chastity belt.

"Would you like me to come back later?"

He was dressed in a silk dressing gown, looking quite dashing physically, but his mortified facial expression ruined the image. I could not help but burst into frenzied laughter over how ridiculous I appeared. He finally smiled at me. When he did, I tossed every prudish act away, dropping the blanket to the floor, exposing myself.

"I could not decide what to wear," I confessed with a giggle. "So I guess I won't wear anything."

I should have experienced shame or embarrassment, but to my surprise, I did not. John was my husband. I wanted to find out what would happen next and if it would make me love or hate him. His gaping stare told me he found my actions shocking. Regardless, I could see he enjoyed my nudity.

"If I ever thought that you possessed a shy bone in your body, you have proven me wrong," he said. His eyes roved up and down my frame and remained upon my breasts for some time. Endowed more than most women, I took solace in the fact that he appeared to approve of their size.

"I realize I look foolish," I admitted, "but I really did not like the gown my mother gave me for tonight. It was not appealing."

"There is nothing foolish about the way you appear now," he said in a sultry voice. "You are beautiful."

As I stood there looking at him with desire, I remembered a scripture. "You will long for your husband, and he will rule over you." At that moment, I understood what it meant. Inside my soul, I ached for him to love me so much that I thought myself close to death.

"Hold me." My request burst from my lips without forethought as a shiver ran down my spine. He slowly stepped forward and stopped only a few inches away. He pulled the sash from his dressing gown, revealing his naked body underneath. My eyelids closed, afraid to see what made a man. John slipped out of the garment, and it brushed my flesh as it fell to the floor. His warm arms encircled my body and pulled me flush against him with a slight jerk. As our skin touched, my body tingled with sensations that I had never experienced before. Finally, I opened my eyes and embraced him in return. He stood motionless.

"Are you going to kiss me?" Why did I have to beg for his every move? I had been taught that it was shameful behavior to be an aggressive woman, but I did not care.

His lips met mine with a kiss void of emotion. My heart's desire burst from my chest like a stream of living water, but he did not drink. Instead, it poured wasted at his feet, untasted, unwanted, and unneeded. Nevertheless, I would not give up until I enjoyed every inch of him, and our marriage had been consummated before God. One way or the other, I would make him mine.

When he released my lips, I took his hands and backed up toward the bed. "Make love to me," I whispered. I sat on the bed and slowly scooted into the middle, holding his hand and pulling him down on top of me. My eyes glanced at his exposed manhood, and I saw what would soon be a part of my body. It did not repulse me as I thought it would. Instead, I finally understood what it meant to be one flesh.

"Please," I begged.

John lowered his body, and I spread my legs apart. I would not close my eyes and drift off to dream about the English countryside. No, I wanted to experience him. He cupped my face in his hands. A moment later, the hardness of his shaft pressed against me, searching and separating until it found its way inside. With a quick push, a searing tear caused me to whimper from the pain. Why hadn't my mother warned me? I cursed her at that second but quickly returned to the reality of John's slow and deliberate movements inside my body.

My arms wrapped around his neck, and I held onto him tightly. "I want to love you," I cried, pulling him close and kissing him. His thrusts increased in intensity and speed.

He pulled away from my lips. "You shouldn't love me," he replied, out of breath. The act of intercourse continued for a few more moments. Finally, in one last deep plunge that brought me discomfort, he grunted. Instinctively, I knew he experienced the pleasure men received from the act. My mother was correct on one point; it did not take long.

When he pulled out of me, a terrible emptiness persisted. My body ached, as did my heart. There had to be more for a woman to enjoy, but I did not know what else to expect. Perhaps this was the curse mentioned in the Bible—bear children in pain and receive no pleasure in conception. Men, on the other hand, were awarded ecstasy. I found the situation rather unfair.

He rolled off me and brought the back of his hand to his forehead. For a few moments, he lay motionless staring at the canopy above. Finally, when his heavy breathing subsided, he spoke.

"I'm sorry for hurting you."

The emotional pain I sensed had wounded me far greater than the soreness between my legs. "It's not your fault that it hurts for a woman to lose her virginity. There are other things in life far more painful." I rolled over on my side away from him. A moment later, he grabbed the corner of the blanket, pulling it over our bodies.

"Are you warm enough?"

My lips pressed together in a pout, and I could not speak. Instead, I mumbled "uh-hum" and found myself drifting off to sleep, wondering why John warned me not to love him.

SEVEN

RETURN TO BLYTHE COURT

Our four-week excursion finished far too soon. John took me to Paris and afterward to Switzerland. My dream of seeing the Continent came to pass, but my hope of winning his heart had not. Even the city of love did nothing to spur romanticism on behalf of my husband. Rather duty and resignation kept his emotions in check and his affections indifferent. I did not speak of love again since he warned me on our wedding night. Instead, I moderated any amorous acts and carefully chose my words as each day passed. My focus turned to the scenery as we traveled.

As a result, each day we spent together seemed like I traveled with a hired companion rather than my husband. By the time we returned home, we had not even forged a close friendship but merely existed as a couple. Nevertheless, I had no complaint about my treatment. John continued to be tender and polite, but I witnessed his attention drift elsewhere as if his thoughts remained in England.

As far as our physical intimacy, he did not seek it as often as I hoped he would. The same scenario continued during each encounter as it had the first night we spent together. I accepted what little he gave, whether it be a kiss or his hands exploring my body. After a few more acts of intimacy, my body adjusted to him quickly, and the pain subsided. Nevertheless, my unfulfilled yearning persisted beyond his usual groan of release. When he pulled out, the aching for more continued. If I had already experienced the totality of what sexual pleasure had to offer a woman, I would soon become my mother drifting off in my mind to the English countryside.

Upon our return to Blythe Court, the entire staff congregated in the entrance hall to welcome our arrival. Since I had not been formally presented to the servants before our wedding, except for Melanie, I paid particular attention to the introductions. The duke and duchess had relocated to their primary estate holdings, leaving John the promised residence. In their absence, I had become the lady of the grand manor house, and it would be my responsibility to oversee the inner workings of the household. The head butler, Mr. Rhodes, reported directly to me, as well as the housekeeper. Thankfully, my mother prepared me for such a task, allowing me to observe as she supervised the domestics at our home.

John, on the other hand, would work closely with the estate manager and game-keeper to attend to his landholdings and finances. Frankly, I hadn't a clue what else he did for work, amusement or entertainment. Another mystery I would need to solve.

We walked down the line of uniformed servants from the housekeeper to the scullery maid. The men bowed, the women curtsied, and I smiled while expressing my pleasure in meeting each of them. Melanie stood in the line as well giving me a warm grin. She glanced at John and quickly pulled her eyes away as if she were shy to be in his presence. He paid no attention to her or to the rest of the staff for that matter, who appeared engrossed in his interaction with me. Eventually, it would become evident to the entire household we were not lovers.

It is merely an arrangement, the words echoed through my mind, which I had spoken to Melanie over a month ago. Now that my life at Blythe Court had begun, I needed to make the most of the years ahead. When our first child arrived, at least I would be able to love someone else. I intended to break the mold of allowing the governess to take all of my children's attention. A gaping hole had been left in my heart, creating a deep-seated need for a purpose to life. I determined to fill it to ease the pain with children and other pursuits.

After the staff dispersed and returned to their duties, John excused himself and headed toward the study to check on estate affairs during our absence. I requested that Melanie help me unpack and get settled in, which she obliged with eagerness.

"You look rested, my lady," she commented.

"Yes, rested."

"May I ask where your travels led you?"

"France and Switzerland," I responded halfheartedly. "I enjoyed the scenery, but we were anxious to return to England."

"That is a shame, my lady. I would have thought your time away would have been more pleasant."

The footmen arrived with my trunk, and Melanie swiftly went into action unpacking. My clothes needed washing, and a few dresses mended. The poor young lady had her chores piled high.

"I am afraid that I tore the sleeve in my blue day dress, being clumsy by snagging it on a chair. You will need to mend it." In retrospect, I must have been terribly distracted because I ruined another dress during our trip. "I also stepped on the hem of my yellow dress and ripped the seam. It was a bumbling honeymoon, to say the least."

"I will take care of it, your ladyship," she replied, examining the damage.

"Would you mind having the chambermaid bring up hot water? It has been days since I bathed."

"Of course," she said.

She scurried from the room to ask for assistance, and I sat down on the bed. My hand slid across the silk coverlet. My new bedchamber, as the lady of the house, had been chosen by John and recently redecorated for my arrival. His nighttime lodgings were in an adjacent room, which frankly broke my heart.

It was not unusual behavior for spouses to keep separate bedchambers, but I hoped he would at least dispense with it early in our marriage. As often as he came to me, getting pregnant would take longer than I wanted.

Dinner between the two of us ended in silence. We barely spoke a word. He asked if my quarters were comfortable, and I praised the décor of the interior. John appeared to fall into a brooding state of mind, so I attempted to make conversation.

"Do you mind if I invite a few lady friends over for tea on Friday?"

"No, of course, not," he replied.

His amicable response gave the impression he felt relieved not having to be in my company. I remained civil but frankly found it challenging. After finishing my last bite, I scooted back the chair and stood to my feet. Surprised at my movement, he frowned with concern.

"I'm tired," I announced. "I want to retire early this evening."

He got up from his chair. "I understand," he replied. "I think I might do the same."

I walked to his side and whispered in his ear. "Might I join you later?"

He pulled away and glanced over at the footman, no doubt worried the man heard my question. "Not this evening," he answered in a low tone. "Perhaps another night."

His spurn tore another piece of my already wounded heart.

"As you wish," I coolly responded. Not wanting to remain for further conversation, I turned and departed. When I made my way to my room, I decided not to ring for Melanie. I was not in the mood to be handled by another person or talk for that matter. Sulking and ruminating over my circumstances seemed far more appealing.

After changing into a nightgown and climbing between the crisp sheets, I covered myself up to my chin with a blanket. The clock chimed nine o'clock, much earlier than my regular time to retire. It was our first night back at Blythe Court as husband and wife, and he would not even share my bed with me. Emotionally drained, I slipped into a restless sleep.

Hours later, my eyes opened. I glanced about in the dark and lonely room and ached to be in John's presence. Why must he push me away? Determined to try once more, I slipped out of bed and wrapped a robe around my chilled body. Surely, he could give me a moment of comfort, even if it were but a simple hug and a peck on the cheek. I could not bear his lack of attention.

Though our rooms joined, I had never seen the inside of his quarters. It wasn't about to stop me, so I softly tapped on the door a few times. To my disappointment, after multiple knocks, he did not answer. Undeterred, I grasped the handle and found it unlocked. I turned the knob and pushed open the door, revealing the interior. He was nowhere in sight, and his bed had not been turned down for the night. Where had he gone?

Confused by his disappearance, I closed the door and decided to wander downstairs to look for him. The entire manor house was a labyrinth of rooms and corridors that I had not yet explored. To help guide my steps, I grabbed a brass candlestick, lit the wick, and proceeded downstairs. One by one, I made my way through the dark entrance hall, the drawing room, the parlor, the library, and then wondered if he were upstairs in the long gallery. Unable to locate John planted a seed of distrust in my heart. I concluded he might be in his private study, so I headed in its direction. Upon my arrival, I found it empty too.

I stood in the doorway pondering his whereabouts, fearful that my next wandering down an unfamiliar hall would result in getting lost. As I turned and glanced down the corridor, I saw him approach, emerging like a ghost out of the darkness. His eyes widened in surprise when he saw me standing there.

"What are you doing out of bed?" he inquired, halting in front of me.

John's clothes looked disheveled and wrinkled, and his hair wild and out of place. He raked his fingers through his unruly locks and smoothed back the stray strands.

"I might ask the same of you," I countered, eying him warily.

"I fell asleep in a chair," he said, shifting in his stance uneasily.

Immediately, I knew that he had lied, as I had just passed every chair in five rooms. My stomach balled into a knot that he had been untruthful to me. Regardless, my longing for him remained.

"I'm lonely, and I wanted to join you in

bed." My admission caught him off guard.

"It's late, you should return to your room," he replied, offering me no comfort or companionship.

"I don't understand why you agreed to marry me," I snapped. "You want absolutely nothing to do with me as your wife. I feel abandoned, unwanted, and despised. Do you want me to leave and go back to my parents? Will that make you happy?"

My voice rose to such a pitch, it echoed down the hallway. I was sure it carried to the servants' quarters. *Let them hear*, I thought to myself. They will see his treatment of me soon enough and add up the sad state of affairs. John's countenance softened undoubtedly from guilt about his behavior. He lowered his eyes and reached out to grab my hand.

"I am sorry," he said with remorse. "Come with me and let's go to bed."

Three words left his lips, which gave me little comfort. He had not expressed any other thought regarding my sensation of abandonment or reason for his behavior. My relationship with John Broadhurst had evolved into a jumbled mixture of love, anger, and suspicion. If I could only come to the point of indifference and accept things as they were, I might be happy with him. However, I did not want to admit defeat in winning his heart. I wanted a husband, a happy marriage, and some sense of belonging.

"Thank you," my voice squeaked out in a whisper. My fingers wrapped around John's hand, and I refused to let go. It was warm to the touch. He gently led me up the stairs. Rather than going to his room, he took me back to mine. I did not care because at least we would be together.

After closing the door, we stood by the bed, and he gazed into my eyes, acting hesitant.

"You can hold me," I said. "It's all I need unless you want more."

"If I hold you through the night in my arms, will that suffice?"

I shook my head, yes. He undressed before me, and we slipped under the covers together. When his arm gathered me and pulled me close, I snuggled my head in the corner of his shoulder and eventually relaxed in his embrace. He gave me a sweet kiss on my forehead and stroked my hair.

"Go to sleep now, Ann. I'm here."

A peaceful and satisfying rest washed over me as I lay in his arms, enjoying the security. If only he would stay with me and not drift away.

EIGHT

THE WAY OF THINGS

A soft knock on the door stirred me from my slumber. My eyelids fluttered, and finally, I awakened to find John still next to me, sound asleep. I glanced at the clock and answered, "yes." To my surprise, the door opened, revealing Melanie with her usual tray of tea and bread she offered upon awakening. Amazed she entered without my final approval, I sat up in bed startled. My movement stirred John, and he rolled over. She saw the two of us in bed and gawked in shock.

"Oh, my goodness," she cried. "Forgive me for the intrusion."

She started to back out of the bedchamber as John bellowed at the top of his voice.

"What the bloody hell are you doing in here? Get out!"

His gruff response to her disturbance

caused Melanie to burst into tears. It shocked me, and I shot him a disapproving glare.

"Come back in a half hour, Melanie, when it is more convenient." She backed out of the room sobbing and closed the door behind her.

"Was that necessary?" I scowled at him. "You scared the daylights out of her."

"She shouldn't barge in like that without being given entrance," he grumbled, throwing the blanket off him and standing up. He snatched his pants from the floor, slipped them on, and grabbed his shirt. "Tell her to make sure she never does that again." John grabbed his remaining clothes, flung open the adjoining door, and banged it shut rattling the picture on the wall.

"Well, put volatile temper on your short list of his emerging personality traits," I grumbled. In spite of everything, his actions were uncalled for, and I patiently waited for Melanie's return. An apology was due. Whether or not my husband would be man enough to offer one, would be interesting to watch. A half hour passed, and a knock came at the door again.

"Come in," I said. To my surprise, one of the chambermaids stood in the doorway.

"Where is Melanie?" I inquired.

"In the servants' quarters, my lady. I am afraid she is crying and embarrassed about having walked in on you and his lordship."

"It was an understandable mistake," I said. "You can put down the tray and leave. Go fetch her to come and attend to my morning needs. She should not fear me, and I am sorry for my husband's outburst."

"Yes, my lady."

The young maid scurried from my room. As I finished my tea, and my lady's maid returned. Her eyes and nose were red from tears.

"I'm so very sorry," she began. Her voice quavered, and she lowered her head peering at the floor rather than at me.

"It is forgiven. Think nothing more of it, and I shall have my husband apologize to you for his burst of anger."

"Oh, please don't, my lady. I deserved it."

"Nonsense," I countered. "Now we will talk no more of it. Help me with my morning toilette and dressing."

I fully intended to make sure John apologized. The home in which I grew up always showed respect to the staff, and I intended to do the same in my household.

Melanie helped me prepare for a busy day. I planned to acclimate myself to the running of the estate by meeting with the butler and head housekeeper. After I dressed and dismissed Melanie to attend to other duties, I descended the stairs and arrived in the dining room. John was nowhere in sight.

"Has my husband been down for breakfast?" I asked Mr. Rhodes upon finding John missing again.

"Yes, my lady. He left to meet with Mr. Williams, the estate manager. They have gone to the cage, I believe, to talk about doing some repairs on the building."

"Did they ride or walk?"

"They usually ride, my lady."

I enjoyed horsemanship. It was apparent John would be away from Blythe Court often on some excuse, and I needed to seek recreation. Besides, I was curious as well about the stables and how many horses John owned.

"Mr. Rhodes, is it possible to have a groom saddle a horse for me as well? I would like to take in a bit of fresh air after breakfast."

"Yes, of course. I will see to it now."

After having a leisurely breakfast and

returning to my suite, I changed into a riding habit and headed out-of-doors. The partly sunny day painted puffy white clouds that swiftly crossed the sky, pushed along by a gusty breeze. As I set out on the estate grounds, I headed for the hill where we enjoyed the picnic on the weekend of the house party. It afforded an exceptional view of the landscape and would be a superb place to spend a few moments in silence and contemplation.

Upon my arrival, I dismounted and tethered the horse to a nearby bush. My hat did little to shade the bright sun from my eyes. I placed my hand above my brow and squinted in the direction of the tower, hoping to see John and Mr. Williams. It would be nice to spend a private moment with him riding if I could convince him to do so.

My eyes focused on the tower where I saw a horse tethered. To my surprise, John stood by his steed, patting him on the neck while waiting for Mr. Williams. A moment later, I saw another person approach from the direction of the residence. Her exuberant step headed straight for John. When I recognized who it was, I brought my hand to my chest, afraid my heart would stop from the shock. As I witnessed them embrace, I staggered backward, nearly fainting. In my husband's arms stood Melanie.

After their brief greeting, John opened the door, and they disappeared inside. My eyes glanced around the landscape, looking for the arrival of Mr. Williams. To my disappointment, he was nowhere in sight. I knew then that John's explanation for his activities that morning had been a lie. In its place, the betrayal of my lady's maid and husband played out before me in vivid detail.

Their clandestine rendezvous, now behind closed doors, could only mean one thing—an intimate encounter. Why else would he have smiled at her after so rudely shouting at her that very morning, and then willingly embracing her with such fervency? What I had witnessed led me to believe that their relationship has surpassed that of master and servant.

Emotionally numb and fearful they might see me, I mounted my horse and sped back to Blythe Court. My astonishment and agony exploded in torrents of tears streaming down my face. The question about his lack of affection had been answered—he loved another woman. Not just any woman but my lady's maid! How long had this affair been brewing? After considering his actions before our marriage and Melanie's envy over our wedding, I gathered the romance had been in place for some time.

"If he loved her so much, why didn't he marry her?" I screamed aloud. My dowry, no doubt. Obedience to his family, afraid of being cut off from his father, the possibilities were endless. John Broadhurst was a coward, liar, and a womanizer.

As I approached Blythe Court, consumed by painful emotions, I halted the horse and tried to compose myself. Two options stood before me. The most obvious would be to dismiss Melanie and have her driven from Blythe Court. Whether that would put distance between the two would be questionable. It would be easy for John to set her up somewhere else as his mistress and continue the tryst regardless of my demands. The second course of action would be to say nothing and bury my pain. Once I became pregnant, perhaps their affair would come to an end, and finally, he would fall in love with me.

While contemplating the sordid state of affairs, my head spun in dizziness. Tortuous imaginations of the two intimately inter-twined filled my mind. No doubt, he satisfied her by making love and not grunting his way through the act as he did with me. The thought of having him revisit my bed made me nauseated. How could I let him touch me knowing he shared his body with her? For that matter, how could I keep her as my lady's maid knowing the deceit she played before me each time we were together?

"Oh, God, I don't know what to do," I cried. My arm clutched my waist from the horrid revelation, and an overwhelming need to return home consumed me. "I need Mother." Whatever wisdom she would give me, I would accept. My soul ached, remem-bering the premonition I had beforehand that John would wound my heart. I had expertly prophesied what I had witnessed this morn-ing.

When I felt assured that my tears had dried and I exhibited an ounce of self-compo-sure, I went directly to the stables, dismounted, and asked for a coach to be brought to me posthaste at the front entrance. I hastily returned to my bedchamber and changed my clothes. Afterward, I descended the stairs and told Mr. Rhodes something of importance had arisen. If the marquess needed to know my whereabouts, he should say to him that I departed to visit my mother. As expected, I received an odd expression about my hasty exodus but felt no need to explain further.

I climbed into the carriage and did not know if I would ever return to Blythe Court. My emotions were a jumbled assortment of shock, hurt, and resentment. A thousand questions haunted me, demanding answers. I hoped that my mother's counsel would give me guidance before I did something rash like killing both of them in their sleep.

As I began the journey, I suddenly feared Mother would not be there. Upon arriving, I sprinted into the manor house where I grew up and ran through the hallways seeking her whereabouts. Thankfully, I found Mother in the parlor, alone, working on her needlepoint. Wishing for privacy, I grabbed the door and banged it shut. My mother jolted in her seat and looked at me startled.

"Good gracious, Ann, what are you doing here?"

My shortness of breath made it nearly impossible to speak. Mother rose to her feet, and I ran into her arms, clinging to her tightly.

"Oh, Mother, the most dreadful thing has happened." I started to cry, expelling my injured heart.

"What happened? Is John all right?" She stepped back and frowned.

"All right?" I heaved out of breath. "He's having an affair with my lady's maid of all people!"

"Oh, dear," she replied, leaving her mouth gaping open. "So early in your marriage?" Mother took my hand and pulled me down next to her on the settee.

So soon? I could not believe my ears. Did she insinuate my horrible marriage had been entirely my fault?

"As far as I can tell, this happened before I married him. Did you know?"

"No, of course not," she swiftly denied. "However, dear," she said in a patronizing voice, "it is not unusual for a husband to stray from the marriage bed."

Her words and nonchalant attitude stung my heart. Seemingly, she thought this situation was an ordinary course of married life. It made me wonder if she had turned a blind eye toward my father's behavior.

"Do you know this from first-hand knowledge, or are you giving me platitudes?" My inquiry had been cruelly articulated, but my mother did not hesitate in answering.

"Yes, I have known for some time your father has engaged in various illicit affairs during our twenty-five-year marriage and keeps a mistress in London even now."

"Dear God, Mother, why do you put up with it?" I stifled a sob.

"And what do you suggest I should have done?" she angrily countered. "You need to understand this is the way things are with men. We give them companionship and children, and they find their entertainment elsewhere."

Mother's eyes pleaded for my understanding instead of judgment, but I struggled, scowling at her in disbelief as she continued.

"I would have ended up destitute and in a workhouse had I left your Father. A woman has no rights to her children either, and I would have never seen you nor your brothers and sisters again. Unfortunately, adultery is not grounds enough for a woman to depart and seek dissolution of the marriage. Your father has never laid a hand upon me in a violent outburst to give me cause otherwise. Only with unwarranted physical cruelty and adultery does a woman have a lawful reason to divorce."

"It shouldn't be the way things are. Women shouldn't be treated as property," I moaned in despair. "If this is marriage, then I despise it!" My hands trembled from anger and heated fire shot through my veins from my raging discontent.

"You are in shock, dear, but in time, you will come to accept it as other women."

"There is no reason why John cannot find love and passion in my bed alone rather than in another woman's arms. The fact that my lady's maid serves me daily with feigned loyalty infuriates me. As soon as my back is turned, she dares to meet with him secretly for an illicit rendezvous." Out of breath and trembling, I paused and inhaled before screaming my sentiments. "I should dismiss her immediately."

"Well, how do you know this is true? Did you see them together?"

"Yes, this morning. They met at the hunting tower, and I saw them embrace and go inside."

"Well, I am sorry to hear of it, Ann. Dismiss her if you must, but if John loves her, he will no doubt put her up somewhere and continue the affair regardless of your actions. My advice is to find other pursuits that will fill your days with things that interest you. To love a man only means heartache. As long as he does not beat you but treats you kindly while providing a home and title, you should be grateful for what you have."

While she lectured me on what I should do, I shut my eyelids and discounted her revolting advice. Her entire thought process sounded ludicrous. Had I been so blind all the years I grew into womanhood, I didn't know this was considered normal marital behavior? Apparently, the scriptures were being made a mockery of by men and women throughout England. How could a lifestyle of adultery be acceptable for husbands, while women must be bound at home, continually pregnant, and left penniless? If I had a prior inkling such dichotomy existed, I would have run off to a nunnery and given up men altogether. I found it intolerable on every level.

"I will never give up on John Broadhurst," I said, angrily standing to my feet. "I will fight for his affections and win his heart if it is the last thing I do!"

"Now, dear..."

"Don't dear me," I snapped. "I came to you for wisdom, but if your advice means I accept his disloyal behavior without batting an eyelash, you do not know your daughter."

As quickly as I had run into the room, I ran out and climbed back into my waiting carriage. I barked at the poor driver to return me to Blythe Court. My heart beat thunderously in my chest in response to the rage swirling through my veins. I remembered Charlene's comment about Lady Whittemore and Sir Riley, which confirmed to me such things occurred and no one cared.

"Well, I care," I said aloud, scowling as I stared out the window at the passing scenery. Somehow I would find the wisdom and means to handle the horrible knowledge of my husband's infidelity. There had to be a way to steal his affections.

By the time the carriage returned mid-afternoon, I had successfully reigned in my wild emotions through sheer determination. I returned to my bedchamber and halted at the threshold, scrunching my hands together in a fist. Next to my bed stood Melanie, laying down my newly mended dresses. I wrestled to keep self-control when I wanted to strike her repeatedly. Unfortunately, my tongue did not find such restraint.

"Oh, my lady," she replied, looking startled by my entrance. "I've repaired the damage to your dresses."

Controlled and with all the dignity I could muster, knowing she must have made love to my husband hours before, I slowly entered. I picked up my blue dress to examine the needlework. The sleeve had been mended, but shabbily as far as I was concerned. When I discovered sloppier hemming on my yellow day dress, I lost composure.

"This is careless work," I snarled. Fuming at Melanie's poor stitching, I ripped the crooked threads from the hem. "If you need more training in sewing, I suggest you speak with Mrs. James on how to improve your skills." After gathering both dresses in my arms, I shoved them back at her in haste. "Return these when they have been properly repaired."

The shocked expression on Melanie's face confirmed I had frightened and wounded her emotions. She blushed profusely. I did not care if I hurt her feelings. At that moment, I wanted to call her vulgar names and slap her face until it stung with pain. Tears threatened to fill my eyes, so I turned my head and instructed her to depart.

"Leave. I wish to be alone," I gruffly demanded.

She said nothing and scurried away. I slammed my door, sat down on my bed, and wept.

NINE

MULTIPLE CHOICES

The circumstances that I faced caused me to reflect upon the person I had become in life. After my marriage and its consummation, I sensed a growing maturity of my personality. My station in life had become one of a wife, marchioness, and mistress of the grand estate in which I lived. Unbeknownst to me, however, my newfound position of responsibility would be severely tested for character and stamina.

Early in my marriage, when I realized John did not love me, I reluctantly accepted my position in his life. Of course, I clung to the hope that one day it would change. Now that I knew his heart unequivocally belonged to another woman, it entirely altered my perspective.

I had been cheated out of love to no fault of my own. The unfairness of my state of affairs presented difficult choices for me to make. Two paths stood before me. I could be a victim or a victor in this complicated scenario. Whether I gained victory out of spite or cleverness would reveal much about my character. I hoped my ingenuity would prevail if I were to keep John from hating me in the end. It would be a delicate task to accomplish because acting spiteful would clearly bring more satisfaction to my wounded heart.

When the dinner hour arrived, I dressed without Melanie's summons for assistance. I feared my raw emotions would strike out, and I needed time to withdraw my claws. John waited for me in the parlor. He held a drink in hand and gazed out of the window when I entered.

"Good evening," I said, walking toward him. No servants were around to find my actions out of place, so I gave him a kiss on the cheek. "How was your day?"

My affectionate display apparently surprised him by the widening of his eyes. Outward exhibitions of affection, even in the home in which I grew up, were considered improper behavior. There were traditions I wished to abolish in my marriage. I saw no harm in expressing endearment toward my husband, within reason, of course.

"Fine," he said, sounding noncommittal.

I wanted to put him on the spot further, so I prodded for more. "Mr. Rhodes told me you and Mr. Williams were at the cage this morning discussing repairs." John pulled his gaze away and took a sip of his drink. I anxiously awaited his lie.

"Yes, the roof needs mending and a few other items."

"Do you intend to use it regularly again for hunting or as the gamekeeper's residence?" I discerned precisely what he used it for but restrained my imagination.

"Simply general repairs," he answered. "And what about you? Mr. Rhodes told me you took an unplanned visit to see your mother today. Is everything all right?"

He finally turned and looked at me. There was not a speck of guilt in his eyes, which I found irritating. Didn't he possess a conscience?

"Oh, yes," I answered, flashing a deceitful smile. "I had an overwhelming urge to share with her our honeymoon and the many places we visited."

"Good. I'm glad to hear of it," he said.

He swallowed my lie, and my deviousness brought me pleasure.

"You know, I have been thinking," I said.

"About what?"

"It might be pleasant to host a small dinner party and invite your friends. I would like to become more acquainted with your social circle." I reached out and touched his forearm to encourage a favorable answer. "Would that be all right?"

"I don't see why not," he said. "We can discuss the guest list tomorrow."

"Excellent," I replied. "By the way, did you apologize to Melanie for snapping her head off this morning? Really, John, I felt terrible for the poor girl."

His actions were suspect, the more I thought about it. No doubt, he wanted to set up some type of stage to show his dislike of Melanie, which made me wonder if they planned the intrusion together. If so, it had been well played on their part.

"Not yet," he mumbled.

"Well, now is as good a time as any." I glanced down the hall and caught sight of the butler. "Mr. Rhodes, might I have a word with you?"

"Yes, my lady?"

"Please ask Melanie to come here to the parlor as soon as possible."

"As you wish," he replied, stepping away to take care of my request.

"What are you doing?" John scowled at me.

"It is obvious unless I give you the opportunity that poor girl is going to continue to be afraid of you. She is my lady's maid, and I would like her to stay and not be frightened away."

The mortified expression on his face gratified me after the pain of infidelity I had endured earlier in the day. When Melanie entered the parlor, he stiffened like a marble statue and turned ashen. She, on the other hand, halted at the threshold, shocked by her summons. Her hands clutched together in front of her waist. Perhaps she feared I had discovered their adulterous affair. I enjoyed the moment immensely, seeing them both in distress during the awkward encounter.

"Melanie, my husband has something he wishes to say to you." John hesitated and shifted his stance. "Go ahead," I encouraged him. After clearing his throat, he looked at

Melanie's apprehensive face.

"I apologize for yelling at you this morning and bringing you to tears," he said in a tremulous voice. "My wife tells me I should have handled the situation differently, and I'm inclined to agree that she is right. I humbly beg your pardon."

Well done, John, I thought to myself. I glanced over at Melanie. A flash of relief eased across her terrified countenance.

"I am sorry for barging into her ladyship's bedchamber. It shall not happen again, your lordship."

"Excellent. The matter is settled," I said, concluding the pained moment. I turned toward Melanie. "You may go now. I will undress this evening on my own and will see you in the morning." I still could not stand the idea of her touching me after being with my husband. Perhaps tomorrow.

She glanced at John and curtsied before me. "Yes, my lady. As you wish."

After she had left the room, I turned my attention to John. "Thank you," I said. "Being kind to the staff has always been a priority of mine. I hope we can agree as husband and wife to treat them with respect because of their loyal service." I purposely emphasized the word "loyal" to make a point.

He downed his drink. "Yes, you are quite right. I agree."

"John, it means a lot to me that we share common ground on one subject." Even though the situation reeked of deceit, I did want to find common ground where we thought alike.

Mr. Rhodes entered the parlor and announced dinner. I stepped forward and wrapped my arm around my husband. He played the role of the attentive spouse and escorted me into the dining room. We spent a leisurely dinner together, chatting about frivolous subjects. The familiar longing for his love swelled in my heart. A part of me wanted to hate him, but I could not. He was my husband, and I determined to fight for him until I won his affections.

John did not visit my bedchamber at night, which I assumed had been due to his sexual satisfaction earlier in the day. I couldn't allow him to touch me—not yet, anyway. The following morning Melanie arrived with a tray in hand and knocked on my door.

"Yes, who is it?"

"It's me, your ladyship," she replied, sounding timid in her voice.

"You may come in."

When she entered the room, I did not want to hate her. It would only consume me instead. Frankly, I could not discern what to feel about Melanie—anger, envy, pity—they were all choices I could make.

"Good morning, your ladyship," she said. She set the tray on my night table. "Mrs. James is helping me with my seamstress skills," she announced. "I should have your dresses returned this afternoon."

"That's fine," I replied. My sharp tone expressed the day before needed an apology as well. "I am sorry for snapping at you, too," I said. "My day yesterday was not the most pleasant."

"Perhaps it will be better today," she said, looking innocent.

I watched her quietly as she went about her duties, getting my clothes ready, and became curious about her past.

"How long have you worked at Blythe Court?"

"Four years," she answered. "Mrs. James hired me as a chambermaid. When you came for the weekend house party, she asked me to be your lady's maid because we were short on staff. It was exciting to be given the opportunity for advancement."

"Well, I am glad you did," I lied. "You did such a splendid job that I insisted you remain." Of course, now I was sorry for having done so.

"It's very kind of you and J—."

Melanie swiftly halted her speech about to express her familiarity with my husband's name.

"And his lordship," she nervously corrected, "to give me this opportunity."

My eyes narrowed at her when she turned her head away from me, no doubt afraid I caught the J-sound on the tip of her tongue. I could not help but wonder why she wanted to be near me. Surely she was tired of waiting upon my every whim. Did John think by putting her right under my nose, I would not suspect they were lovers? How could she serve me each day knowing that I married the man she adored? Her reasoning baffled me.

My countenance fell into a sullen pout. I

wanted to dismiss Melanie from my employment. It would be far better for me if he set her up in some fancy townhome. Henceforth he could go to her on the sly for his sexual trysts, rather than doing so in broad daylight in front of the entire staff. I could not help but wonder how many were aware of their shameful affair.

Nevertheless, I could not—not yet, anyway. I needed her close so that I could discover why John loved her and what hold she kept upon him that I did not possess. Were they more passionate together in bed? Did she provide him sexual pleasure in areas that I knew nothing about? Perhaps he adored her because of her sweet and unpretentious disposition. Wasn't my personality pleasant enough to gain his affection? Oh, God, I wanted to hate her because she possessed John's heart when it should be mine. Anxiousness sucked the breath out of my lungs, and I felt as if I were suffocating.

"Shall I have the chambermaid bring water up for a bath this morning, my lady?"

"Yes, please do," I said. After taking my last sip of tea, I slipped out of bed and glanced at my adjoining door to John's room. I never entered his bedchamber in the morning and wondered if his valet were tending to him at the same moment. Unfortunately, the gentleman who served his needs was older and unattractive. My vindictive state of mind regretted the fact he was not young and virile. I could have an affair with him while my husband enjoyed my lady's maid. I knew I could never do such a thing, but the malicious thought pleased me. In the meantime, my thoughts began to formulate another avenue for spiteful amusement.

TEN

THE DINNER PARTY

We reviewed the guest list for our first dinner party as a married couple. Afterward, I met with the cook to discuss the menu. Mr. Rhodes and Mrs. James assured me the staff would do a superb job for my first gathering as a hostess.

When the evening arrived, the dining room glowed with silver candelabras, shiny English bone china, and polished cutlery. My new position as head of the household brought a deep sense of accomplishment. At least in one area of my life, I could lift my chin with pride.

John never spoke of his like or dislike of his father's gift of Blythe Court upon our marriage. Perhaps the estate had been far too familiar for him to express any partiality toward the grand house. Nevertheless, the structures and impressive grounds said much about our status in society. Little did others know, or so I hoped, that it held a dark secret of immorality behind its doors.

The guests for the evening consisted of Charlene, who arrived with her new fiancé, Robert Wellington, approved by her parents. She recently traveled from London to Kenwood Hall, not far from Blythe Court, for a holiday. Evidently, she had decided not to run away with the penniless love of her life, Mr. Brighton.

I found it odd, frankly, thinking she would be better off to marry for affection. Maybe poor men were not as adulterous as the wealthy aristocracy. My mind drifted back to the comment John made about their affections and the poverty she would endure if she married him. He called it a family scandal when he had perpetrated one of his own. I believed him a hypocrite and now wondered if he spoke of it for some purpose. Little did I realize beforehand that a scandal already brewed at Blythe Court. I couldn't help shake the notion Charlene might be privy to my husband's choice of a lover and remained sympathetic toward him.

John also invited other acquaintances who I only met briefly in the reception line at our wedding. Percy Kent, an unattached aristocratic bachelor, arrived without a lady to accompany him to dinner. He was an acquaintance of John's from university, whose friendship had continued. His gregarious attitude brought a breath of fresh air into my dismal home. I found myself immediately drawn to his charisma. As far as the other couples, they were individuals or couples that John had been acquainted with through his family, most of whom I decided were dull. My husband did not appear particularly close to any of them, and they reminded me of cardboard figurines, filling the empty seats around the table.

When dinner began, Percy sat next to me. We swiftly struck up interesting conversations. He possessed a knack for making me laugh, which apparently John did not find amusing by the strained look upon his face. He kept glancing and the two of us chatting like old friends. Percy eventually turned his attention to my husband.

"John, married life seems to agree with you. I dare say you are a lucky man to have such a beautiful and stimulating woman for a wife. Well, done!"

Percy flashed a flirty wink, and I responded with a broad smile. I could have kissed him for prodding John.

"I don't think he knows how lucky he really is," I added, raising a brow. John looked at me in the eyes and then glanced at Percy.

"Oh, I do," John interjected, trying to save face. "She is indeed an exceptional lady."

He smiled at me warmly, but I knew it to be a show of fondness rather than an actual act of love.

"You better be good to her, or I shall sweep in like a hawk and steal her away."

The rascal peeked at my bosom, indicating his appreciation for my endowed state. At last, a man who flattered me and gave me an ounce of attention. My starved ego eagerly drank of every indecent glimpse. When I glanced back at John, his countenance radiated his acute displeasure over the flirtatious banter. I had hoped the evening would afford me such a situation, so I grabbed the opportunity and continued to tease Percy.

After dinner, we all departed to the large sitting room for amusement. Percy pulled me away for a game of cards while the others began their guessing game of charades. John occasionally glanced in my direction, watching me like a hawk.

"So, tell me truthfully, Ann, is he treating you well?" Percy asked in all seriousness. His eyes narrowed with concern.

His question startled me, but I gave a straightforward answer. "The man is a mystery to me, but yes, he treats me kindly."

"Kindly, you say? Oh, how boring," Percy snickered. "If you were my wife, there would be many feisty encounters between us, I assure you, and not an ounce of boredom."

"You flatter me," I said, batting my eyelashes and glancing at those nearby. "Lower your voice or people will wonder if you are proposing indecent engagements between us."

"Then I shall be indecent as possible. If you tire of him," Percy said, reaching over and touching my hand, "I can be extremely inconspicuous."

Ah, yes, there was that word again. It was perfectly acceptable to have affairs if everything played out discreetly. I honestly wondered if John cared if I took a lover.

"I do not believe John would be too happy should he find out," I replied, trying to dismiss the proposal. "Besides, I thought there was a double standard when it came to infidelity in marriage. It is acceptable for men to find pleasure outside the marriage bed but inexcusable for women to partake of the forbidden fruit."

"You are quite mistaken, my dear. I know plenty of married ladies who like fruit," he replied in a sultry voice, making me blush.

"I'm sure you do, Percy," I said with a sly grin. My next words were interrupted by the arrival of John at our side. Apparently, he had been watching our private conversation.

He bowed down and whispered his displeasure in my ear. "Don't you think you are ignoring the other guests?"

"Not really," I answered in a low voice. "I am quite entertained, but if you insist we play a game of charades together, I am sure Percy and I can oblige."

"Charades?" Percy replied enthusiastically. "Yes, let's play." He stood to his feet, offered me his hand, and I gladly took it since my husband had not the good sense to offer his. I flashed John a sardonic smile as we passed by, witnessing his irritation. *Good, I thought. A prick of jealousy is just what you need.*

My evening turned out to be an educational and enjoyable experience. Percy provided much-needed laughter in my life while my husband displayed a welcome hint of possessiveness. Whether his emotion came from an ounce of affection for me or sheer irritation, I had yet to discover. Perhaps I wounded his self-worth, acting as if I might consider someone else more attractive and interesting. Nevertheless, as we said goodbye to our guests and made our way to our bedchambers, our time together burst into a heated exchange.

"I found your behavior this evening with Percy inappropriate," he grumbled in a throaty voice.

"Inappropriate?" I innocently responded. "In what way?" We stood outside of my bedchamber glaring at one another.

"You appeared to welcome his flirtatious behavior, which embarrassed me in front of my guests. Others perceived it as well."

"I did welcome it," I curtly replied. "You barely give me the time of day in our marriage, let alone look at me with any desire or want." I was becoming irate, and I balled my fists together at my sides. Oh, how I wanted to beat him on his chest repeatedly until I expelled all the pain over his affair.

"Obviously, I should attend to you this evening," he said, moving closer to me. His hand reached behind me, turned the doorknob to my room, and pushed it open.

"Oh, now you want me because another man expressed his interest?" I said, seething between my teeth.

"It's evident I have been neglectful in this area," he replied with his eyes narrowing into threatening slits.

He pulled me by my hand into the room and closed the door behind us. The disdainful countenance frightened me, and I wondered if he intended to rape me to make a point. I didn't want him to treat me with disrespect and force himself upon me, so I tempered my irritation.

"You neglect me," I whispered, my voice trembling and submissive. My lips pushed out into a pout, as I stepped toward him and put my arms around his neck. The conflicted glance in his eyes gave me hope that inwardly, he harbored a small amount of fondness toward me. I leaned forward and kissed him, but the hollowness behind his response persisted.

"Make love to me," I whimpered. "Please, John, you never give me enough of you."

"Don't ever act that way again," he warned in a stern voice. "You are my wife and the future Duchess of Dorset. It's unbecoming."

"Then treat me like your wife," I said. "Pay attention to me."

John spun me around and released my body from my dress. It pooled at my feet in a heap, and when I turned around, the agitation burning in his eyes remained. He intended to teach me a lesson. After John stripped me naked, he backed me up to the bed, and I willing reclined. He untied his ascot, then threw off his tailcoat, vest, and linen shirt. A moment later, he undid his trousers, exposing his bulging shaft. His dark eyes glowered at me with authority and domination.

"You are correct," he remarked in a husky voice. "You are my wife." Parting my legs, he lowered himself and swiftly slipped inside of me. I gasped at his entrance, making a claim of ownership to my body. No kisses or whispered words of affection accompanied his carnal need. He speedily took what belonged to him, while jealousy burned into my soul as he heartlessly thrust himself until satisfaction arrived. He deposited his seed and left me longing and aching for more. It never changed, and I loathed him for it. Surely, Melanie received the totality of his passion and love, while I, on the other hand, received his domination.

When he finished his task of putting me in my place, he surveyed my disheveled state. The smug look of a conqueror gazed down upon me. He had callously used me to make a point, but the thought of him departing me to be left alone for the night became unbearable.

"Stay with me tonight," I pleaded, "and sleep with me." He regarded me with resistance. "I apologize for my behavior," I said, acting remorseful, though inwardly I hailed my ability to move him to jealousy. "It won't happen again." Inhaling a shaky breath, I spoke what he wanted to hear. "You are right, John, I am your wife. I belong to you."

To my relief, he lay alongside and gathered me in his arms. The abrupt actions turned to tenderness. Tonight he would share my bed, and I determined to take whatever morsel he willingly gave.

We slept soundly together in each other arms. When morning arrived, the usual knock came at the door from Melanie. I forgot she existed whenever John spent time with me.

"Wait a minute," I called out.

John stirred, and I nudged him gently. "My lady's maid is here with my morning tea. You should withdraw to your room."

He flipped back the blanket and rose to his feet. Panicked, he grabbed his clothes strewn over a nearby chair and his shoes on the floor.

"Thank you," I said, looking at him with an appreciative glance. "May I have a quick kiss before you depart?"

He shot an observable uneasy glance at the door and back at me. "Of course." John leaned over, gave me a peck on my lips, and afterward disappeared into his bedchamber.

"You may come in now," I called.

Melanie opened the door but appeared hesitant to enter. She must have known John had spent the night in my bed. She set the tray down on my night table and bent over picking up a stocking that he had dropped.

"You had a visitor last night?"

The inappropriate tone of her voice startled me. I refused to answer her inquiry. "You may place it on the chair," I instructed. "I will give it to my husband later."

She obeyed, but her demeanor exuded a loathsome attitude. Did she harbor resentment because I stole a moment from her lover? My eyes narrowed at her for having the nerve to complain.

"Did you have a pleasant dinner party last evening?" she inquired in a more amenable tone.

"Yes, very nice," I responded. I took a few sips of tea but had no appetite.

I allowed Melanie to help me dress for the day. She remained silent for the remainder of her few minutes with me before departing for other duties. Did she finally run out of patience, perchance, serving me daily? After finishing my hair, I dismissed her from my room.

"That is all," I said. "I can take care of the rest."

"Yes, my lady," she said, giving me a half-hearted curtsy. She picked up the breakfast tray, with my empty teacup, uneaten bread, and departed.

Today I would give her more competition for my husband's affection.

ELEVEN

PASSION REALIZED

I descended the stairs and found John at the dining room table. It was unusual for him to join me for breakfast.

"No meetings this morning with Mr. Williams?" I asked, hoping he was taking a break from Melanie.

"Not today," he replied, glancing at me with a curious look.

"What are you staring at?" I flashed a teasing smile in his direction.

"You," he said. "I don't always take the time to tell you how beautiful you are."

I nearly gasped over the compliment but decided it probably came forth due to lingering jealousy over Percy's attention toward me.

"Thank you," I replied. After gathering a small portion of breakfast, I sat across from him at the dining room table. He acted more attentive towards me, occasionally glancing at me with a warm smile.

"Would you like to go for a morning ride on the estate grounds?" he suddenly asked.

I literally choked on my tea after inhaling a surprised breath. After coughing until my airway cleared, I opened my mouth to respond. He smirked.

"Yes, that sounds delightful," I answered.

"Good. I will instruct the groom to saddle the horses and will meet you at the stables in a half hour. Is that enough time?"

"Oh, more than sufficient." My excitement radiated from my voice and face. Giving my husband a bit of rivalry seemed to have stirred his interest in me much more. I played my card well.

He departed the table, and I quickly ate my breakfast. After changing into my riding habit, I met John at the stables. My tailored skirt and jacket accented my figure and tiny waist. I wore a dark purple fabric. A matching lady's top hat, with a black veil that covered my eyes, added to the alluring picture. When he saw me approach, he smiled approvingly.

"You should be aware that I'm a good rider," I warned, mounting my horse. He had never witnessed my horsemanship skills before, and I intended to display my abilities.

"Are you?" he replied, sounding as if he questioned my boasting.

"Even at full speed." My arrogant voice stated my claim, and I caught him off guard by taking the lead with one wallop of my crop. A second later, I was galloping across the green acreage, leaving my husband to dodge the clods of dirt flying up from the hooves of my stallion. I glanced over my shoulder and saw him whip his horse into a frenzy until he caught up to my side.

"To the cage," he yelled, suggesting a destination.

"The first one there is the winner," I challenged in return.

We both laughed aloud, speeding across the landscape. Giddy and out of breath, he won by a short distance. I hated being defeated but enjoyed the look of victory on his face.

"You are quite the rider," John admitted. He dismounted and held out his hand to me.

"There are many things you have yet to discover about your wife, John Broadhurst." I jumped down in front of him. We stood face to face, and for the first time in our marriage, I saw a spark of pleasure in his eyes.

"I have much to offer you if you will only open your heart and take it," I whispered. It was a foolish thing to say, but it must have touched his emotions. He pulled me next to his body and kissed me, nearly knocking off my hat. I relished the sincere, intimate moment, holding onto it like a treasure. If his affection faded again, I would tuck it in the corner of my memory and resurrect the taste of his lips, his strong arms around me, and the look in his eyes.

"What now?" I asked innocently.

"Do you want to go inside?"

The enticing gaze of his sparkling eyes weakened my knees, and my stomach tightened into a knot. The prospect of what could happen between us as husband and wife conflicted with the secrets that lay behind the door. Why did he want me to partake in their clandestine meeting place? The more I pondered it, I knew he chose to commit disloyalty against Melanie, so I gladly allowed him to carry out his betrayal.

"Yes, of course." I held his hand, we entered, and he shut the door. The only light that filtered in came through the cracks of the closed shutters. Even in the dim surrounds, I could see the need in his eyes. He wanted me.

"I will let you take me, John Broadhurst," I said in a sultry voice. "On one condition."

"And what would that be?" he asked. The corner of his mouth raised in a mocking grin.

At that moment, I realized this would be my chance to take from him what I always wanted.

"You might find this surprising, your lordship," I said, teasing him by running the tip of my finger across his bottom lip. "But your wife has needs too."

A brow arched above his right eye. "Needs? Elaborate for me," he replied.

He apparently knew exactly what I meant by his teasing tone. "I want to experience passion," I said, proclaiming my unfulfilled desire. "I'm tired of being denied pleasure. Surely, there must be more for a woman to enjoy in bed, and I want you to show me exactly what it is."

Amusement curled his lips into a wicked grin. "Are you sure that is what you want from me?"

"Yes, you are my husband." Narrowing my eyes at him at threatened, "I swear I will lock you in this tower until you give me what

I want." I giggled over my taunt.

"Very well," he said, surrendering to my demands. "Far be it from me to deny you pleasure, my lady."

What transpired next caught me off guard. My docile husband transformed into a devouring animal. He grabbed me by the waist and pulled me to his lips, forcing his tongue inside my mouth. Shocked by his action, I never imagined a man would do such a thing. Once again, I cursed my ignorance and moaned at the onslaught of sensations. His hand came to my breast and squeezed it tightly. I felt the hardness of his erection press against my pelvis, causing me to ache with need.

As I continued to whimper at his touch, he unbuttoned my jacket and pulled my chemisette from my skirt. A moment later, he methodically stripped me to my corset and petticoat, teasingly kissing my body with each movement.

Undeterred by his actions, I reached out and placed my hand on the bulging manhood hidden in his trousers. I wanted to feel his need for me and hold him in my hand. Surprised I had done so, he breathed heavily into my ear.

"That's a dangerous thing to do to a man, madam," he slurred. "Very dangerous, indeed."

Dangerous or not, I didn't care. After fumbling with his buttons, I released him into my hand. He moaned at my touch, which didn't last long. Suddenly, he lifted me up and carried me up a flight of stairs and kicked open the door to the bedroom. Now I had a chance to defile the same spot Melanie used to take my husband. His face showed no shame but only heated desire.

He laid me on the bed, parted my legs, and slipped his fingers into my moistness. A second later, his tongue found its way into my mouth, kissing me deeply while he fondled me with expert precision. The glorious touch consumed my body, driving me to a heightened sense of insatiable craving. Such pleasure was more than I ever imagined. I moaned between his kisses, engorged with the need for him to fill me. He abruptly pulled away, looking at me with a wicked grin, like an evil rogue about to seduce me beyond my wildest dreams.

"Do you want more?" John eyed me deliciously like a meal.

"Yes," I whined, hoping he would slide himself into me. However, he had other plans, and slowly slipped down between my legs and began a journey with his tongue in places I thought his mouth should never touch. Utterly shocked he had done so, I lost all reason to protest as he sucked and massaged me with his lips and tongue. The nerves in my body tingled like sparks, and a growing fullness demanded release. He continued unrelentingly with his skills I knew never existed. With one more expert movement on his part, I found myself transported into such bliss, I cried my delight, filling the tower with my screams. At last, I had tasted sweet and satisfying pleasure. It was glorious.

As I writhed until it subsided, John repositioned himself upon me. A smug look of victory crossed his face as he slipped inside. His previous slow and tedious movements turned into thrusts sending me into another powerful rise of ecstasy. He placed the palm of his hands beneath me and pulled me upward, releasing a final plunge into my body. Only this time, no grunt came from his mouth. A surge of utter satisfaction roared from his throat. When it ended, I lay exhausted.

We lingered in each other's arms for some time, silently side by side. My head found a familiar place on his shoulder. The touch of his warm skin next to my body brought comfort. For the first time since we married, I actually felt like his wife.

"Why haven't you done those things to me before?" I whispered. My heart knew why, but I wanted to hear what he would say. A few moments passed, and his hand gently stroked my arm back and forth as if he were pondering a response.

"I've been selfish, I suppose," he softly spoke in a repentant tone.

His confession touched my heart. "I hope you never stop," I replied, wishing I could tell him that I loved him. Instead, I remained silent because I feared to lose whatever ground I had gained. He chuckled.

"Pleasure is like opium," he announced, "I am fearful I will turn you into an addict."

"Then, please do." I rolled over and straddled myself across his body. "Are there other positions you can teach me too?"

"You surprise me, Lady Broadhurst," he quipped. "Most wives are frigid creatures scared to explore the depths of pleasure. Didn't your mother condemn sexual inclination to you as a young lady?"

"I am not like others," I heatedly responded. "Besides, who told you wives were frigid and did not wish to enjoy the passions of the marriage bed?"

"My father," he said.

"Oh, dear God," I broke out laughing uncontrollably.

"What's so funny?" He looked at me cock-eyed.

"It appears our parents have duped us both. My mother gave me no instruction except to lie back, open my legs, and think of the English countryside."

He roared with hilarity and reached out with his hands and grabbed my breasts, playfully squeezing my nipples.

"Apparently we have been horribly misled," he replied. "I do admire your breasts, by the way."

John pulled me forward and captured my mouth. The position of my body made a perfect entrance, which he swiftly took advantage of, causing me to gasp aloud.

"Now it's your turn to do what you wish to me," he whispered hotly into my ear. He thrust upward, and I responded with movement.

"Don't stop," I begged, enjoying another moment of intimacy.

"I won't until you fill the tower with your screams again. You shrieked quite loudly, by the way."

His face turned serious, as he began to return me to a place of delight. I knew then he would be my opiate for the rest of my life. If I could keep him captive in my bed alone, I hoped he would never stray. As long as I learned the art of giving him pleasure, I had a chance.

Two hours later, John and I returned to the estate, both of us glimmering like satisfied fools. Unfortunately, I felt nauseated, so I headed to my bedchamber to rest before dinner. When I entered, I found Melanie looking through my jewelry box. I halted in the doorway with my mouth gaping open in disbelief. She did not hear me, so I stood there as she played with my accessories. My patience expired, and I made my presence known.

"What are you doing?" I said, storming into my room. In her hand, lay my ruby necklace John had given me for our wedding.

"Oh, my lady, I am so sorry," she said, putting it back and slamming the lid shut. "They are so beautiful I got carried away admiring your gems."

Her face blushed profusely, and my resentment toward her heatedly rose. I wanted to hurt her, so I did.

"I don't ever want to catch you handling my things again without my permission, do you understand?" She took a step back from me.

"Yes, my lady," she replied, lowering her eyes. She turned to run toward the door, but I halted her departure. "Have the chambermaids bring up hot water for a bath," I said. "I am dusty after a morning ride with my husband to the cage."

Melanie's countenance paled, and I could see the wound I inflicted upon her heart. Instead of acting merciful, I turned the blade further, which I expertly plunged to add to my spitefulness. "I am exhausted from our intimate dalliance behind closed doors," I said, snickering. When I saw the wretched expression on her face, I feigned my apology. "Oh, forgive me." My fingers lifted the veil from my eyes, and I removed my hat. "My comment is most inappropriate. I beg your pardon."

Speechless and unable to respond, Melanie curtsied and left the room. I closed my eyes ashamed over what I had done. Frankly, I never treated anyone so cruelly in my entire life as I did at that moment. Perhaps I had succeeded in pounding a wedge between her and John, which might cause permanent damage.

While waiting for the bath water, I sat on the edge of my bed, queasy and lightheaded. Intermittent pain cramped my stomach. My mother told me that I might be ill during early pregnancy. Even though I wanted to vomit, a part of me became excited that I could be carrying John's child. I only hoped that the dreadful unsettled stomach would not last for months on end.

Twelve

Trip to London

My life with John took on a new dimension each day. Melanie, on the other hand, changed into a sullen and detached servant. I anticipated John's time with her had faded into obscurity, but I possessed no proof that was indeed the case. Because his attention toward me deepened, I felt encouraged. Battles had been won, but the war for his heart still raged.

As our intimacy improved, I yearned to become pregnant. I harbored a secret fear if he still visited Melanie's bed, she might win the blessing that should be mine. I wanted her to remain barren, for dealing with a child between the two of them would undoubtedly be more than I could handle.

Nevertheless, as the weeks passed, I noticed my health deteriorating. Headaches, nausea, and fatigue became part of my morning routine. I began to suspect that I might be pregnant because my menses had not arrived on time either. In my heart, I knew if I could give him an heir, it would undoubtedly win his love.

Not wishing to tell him until I was sure, I asked if he had any objection to my going to London on a shopping spree. My intent was not to procure a new dress but to visit a physician. I feared that if I sought medical attention in Dorchester, he would somehow hear about my visit.

I hated to leave the estate for an extended period because I worried that he and Melanie would take the opportunity to be together. Every day I lived with little knowledge regarding their current relationship. It had been impossible to snoop around and follow him wherever he went. I did take note, nevertheless, of his excuses to meet with Mr. Williams and to ride off somewhere on his fourteen hundred acres to talk about business. Daily I wrestled with the pain of betrayal while clinging to the hope of newfound loyalty.

After convincing myself that I had to take the risk and leave Blythe Court, I made the suggestion during dinner.

"Do you mind if I take a short trip to London? I would like to see my former seamstress for a new dress."

"London?" He raised his head and looked at me. "Why there? Can't you shop in Dorchester?"

"Well, I could," I began, sounding like a spoiled child, "but the best fashions are in London. I will merely be gone for one night." The thought of being away increased the queasiness in my stomach. Would they meet in the tower? Would she come to his bedchamber? Would he go to her? I could easily drive myself insane speculating.

"Where will you stay? I don't particularly care for you traveling by yourself." He frowned at me as if he did not trust or approve of my leaving.

"Do you think your cousin Charlene might put me up for the night?" I hadn't thought of it before until I noticed his resistance to my suggestion.

"Well, I suppose you can take the train. The trip takes three hours, you know, from here to London. I can write ahead that you are coming, but I want confirmation first they can accommodate your arrival."

"Of course, John," I agreed, slightly irritated by the wait. Nevertheless, I did not want to argue lest he changed his mind.

I dabbed my lips with a napkin and glanced up to catch him staring at me. "I'm surprised you haven't asked me for any money," he grinned. "How will you fund this shopping spree of yours?"

The devilish look in his eyes was playful. I had not even thought of asking for money, thanks to my mind being muddled with deceitful plans.

"Would fifty pounds be too much?" I scrunched my shoulders, bracing myself for his answer.

"By the time you pay for your train ticket, transportation in London, and shopping, you'll return with a few crowns in your purse." He pondered for a moment, then continued. "Two hundred pounds should be adequate, on one condition."

"And what would that be?"

"Purchase something in red," he said. "It's my favorite color, but you never wear it."

I brought my hand to my mouth and snickered about the suggestion. "Oh, I think that can be arranged, your lordship." My eyes expressed love while he reflected a hint of affection. Within the next week, I hoped to be in London.

Charlene met me at the station. Though we had not formed any type of friendship, I wished to try to forge one during my short stay. To my disappointment, however, I did not sense she necessarily shared the same wishes.

After I had disembarked, we gave each other a traditional greeting, hugging for a mere second.

"How was your trip?" she asked.

"Pleasant," I replied. It had been a tiring journey, and my body ached with exhaustion. Her driver carried my suitcase and led us outdoors to a waiting carriage.

"John wrote that you wanted to go shopping. Don't you have a seamstress in Dorchester?"

"Not really," I sighed. "I have not made any regular trips into town to look for one, frankly." I remembered Melanie's poor skills and decided to bring her name up into the conversation for a reaction. "My lady's maid, I'm afraid, does not possess any talents as a seamstress. I asked her to mend a few rips in my dresses, and the outcome was disastrous."

"I'm not surprised," Charlene said. "From what I understand, she's always been a chambermaid at Blythe Court. To be honest, I was surprised John allowed her to serve you at all."

"Well, it was not his doing," I clarified. "She helped me during the weekend house party. I found her to be delightful and asked if she would attend me after the wedding."

Charlene did not respond but appeared to ponder my explanation. We climbed into the carriage and shortly thereafter arrived at her residence.

"Mother and Father are away, so it is only the two of us," she said. "I hope you do not mind."

"No, that is fine."

"Follow me, and I'll show you to your room."

Charlene led the way upstairs. As she walked before me, I sensed an unhappy young woman. She had scarcely smiled since my arrival. Whether she disliked me or something else weighed heavily upon her heart, I could not tell. I hoped that after dinner, we might have a long talk and become better acquainted.

"You should be comfortable here," she said, opening the door and leading me into a bedchamber. The footman set my suitcase down and departed.

"If there is anything you need, let me know," she offered. "Do you plan on shopping this afternoon?"

"No, I planned to shop in the morning. I do, however, have an appointment at three o'clock with an old friend that I promised to meet for tea."

"Oh," she replied, looking at me strangely.

"I would invite you to come, but I am afraid we would bore you with our childhood stories. We grew up together." The lies poured from my lips without an ounce of remorse.

"That is quite all right. We can talk at dinner, and I will suggest some dress shops for you to visit in the morning."

"Thank you for understanding, Charlene. I do not wish to injure your spirits since you have been so hospitable to put me up for the night."

"Think nothing of it," she replied.

Her sincerity was palpable, so I quickly pushed aside any guilt. At three o'clock, I would visit Dr. Branson, who had been my family's medical practitioner on previous occasions while in London. I had written ahead of time and secured an appointment. Anxious to discover if I carried John's child, I unpacked and readied myself.

"How many menses have you missed, Lady Broadhurst?" Dr. Branson asked as I lay on the table while he examined me.

"Two." I glanced at the nurse who watched me endure the embarrassing parting of my legs and intimate parts.

"Any other symptoms?"

"I have been exhausted of late and experiencing nausea, abdominal pain, and headaches," I said.

"And you are sexually active with your spouse, I take it?"

I thought it a ludicrous question but responded. "Yes, of course."

"And is he monogamous with you?"

I nearly shot up from the table. "Do you mean is he having an affair?"

"I know it is not a question wives like to discuss, but it helps to identify the possibility of syphilis."

Syphilis? My mouth gaped open. I had never considered such a dreadful diagnosis. My eyes stung with tears considering the horrifying possibility.

"You mean I could be infected?" He did not immediately reply as he continued his internal examination. The possibility of such a terrible thing actually made me tremble.

"You may sit up now," he said, finishing his inspection. He looked at me with concern. "The good news is you are clean from infection. I see no indication of syphilis."

I heaved a sigh of relief. "Oh, dear God, thank you," I mumbled, closing my eyes in relief. "Am I pregnant?"

He shook his head negatively. "At this early stage, it is challenging to ascertain if you are pregnant by mere examination. If you are, by the third month of missing your menses, you should notice a slightly rounded abdomen. You say you have no increased appetite, but a lack of one?"

"Yes, that is true."

"Honestly, I doubt you are. Upon my examination, I observed your uterus is tilted. This often contributes to an inability to conceive."

"You mean I might not be able to get pregnant?" My heart sank in despair.

"Not necessarily, but I am pleased to say that it is not always the case. Certain positions between your husband and yourself might aid in conception."

Even though he left me with a spot of hope, I found it to be of little comfort.

"Since you are not pregnant, we are faced with the mystery of the origin of your headaches, stomach pain, and fatigue. Can you tell me when you first noticed these symptoms?"

My mind wandered back counting the weeks. "A little over a month ago in the morning after my tea and bread."

He stroked his chin and thoughtfully stood there gazing at me. "Let me see your hands," he asked.

Even though I thought his request odd, I held out both of my hands palms up. He turned them over and carefully studied my nails.

"Hum," he mumbled, looking at each finger. His brow creased with concern.

"Hum, what?"

"You see these white lines on your nails?" he asked. He pointed to them with his index finger.

"Yes, I have noticed them of late. What does it mean?" I pulled my hands back and clasped them together in my lap.

"You say you live at Blythe Court outside of Dorchester. Has anyone tested your water supply in the past year?"

"Well, I don't know," I replied, scrunching my brow. "It is an old estate and dates back to the thirteenth century. What in the world does our water supply have to do with my nails?"

"There could be arsenic in your well water or some other type of heavy metal, which produces the same kind of symptoms. The fact you have missed a few menses is not unusual if your body has ingested anything out of the ordinary."

"But no one else has been sick," I countered. My response caused me to pause as I tried to deduce its origins.

"Well, small doses can cause these minor

symptoms, but if they persist over a longer period, it could lead to an unpleasant and painful death."

My mouth gaped open, and I swore my heart stopped beating. I could not speak as my mind drifted to Melanie, who brought my morning tea and bread. Could she be responsible? Had my plan worked so well, she needed to do away with me entirely to keep John?

"And what about your bedchamber, Lady Broadhurst? Does it have green wallpaper?"

"No, it has wood-paneled walls," I replied. "Why are you asking about the color of my wall coverings?"

"The green pigment in wallpaper contains arsenic. Some of my patients have seen significant improvement in their health by getting rid of the wallpaper in their homes."

"And where else can it be found?"

"It is readily available for purchase from any druggist."

I barely knew anything about arsenic or how it could be easily obtained.

"Well, if the source is not from the wallpaper," he continued, "I would suggest you have the water supply tested. If you have any green dresses, you can test if the pigment coloring has arsenic by dropping a small amount of ammonia on the fabric. If it turns blue, arsenic is present in the dye, and you should destroy the dress."

"Anything else?"

"If symptoms become precariously acute, you should seek medical attention immediately."

For a brief moment, I stared at the white lines on my nails. "Isn't arsenic also used to murder people?" I innocently asked, looking at my physician. My tongue articulated the shocking thought floating through my mind, as I tried to process how I had been exposed.

Dr. Branson had a hearty laugh at my expense, as well as the nurse in the room. Apparently, they found my question quite humorous.

"In murder mystery novels," Dr. Branson said, grinning. "I have yet to meet anyone who has actually used arsenic to kill one of my patients."

His calm voice indicated he had not taken my question seriously, but his smile faded. My countenance betrayed the terrifying thoughts running around in my brain.

"Are you suggesting your husband might be trying to kill you?"

I quickly dismissed his assumption. "Oh, absolutely not," I emphatically declared. "We are in love. I do suppose I am prone to be caught up in sensational storytelling. It is all the rage with the ladies these days."

"Oh, yes, I know very well. My wife regularly reads short stories in The Strand Magazine regarding murders being investigated by Scotland Yard and women poisoning their husbands. I have no idea what all the fuss is about." He bellowed a hearty laugh. "Maybe I should worry that my wife wishes to poison me."

Though Dr. Branson thought lightly of the possibility, I could not shake off an ominous sense, thinking of Melanie.

"Frankly, I am worried," I said, showing him my concern.

"Try a process of elimination, and that should lead you to the cause. My suggestion would be to drink more wine and dispense with anything brewed with your water supply, such as tea and coffee, and see if it helps to minimize the symptoms."

Process of elimination. It sounded like a

wise course of action. I would refuse my morning tea and bread.

"Well, if the poisoning stops will I recover and the symptoms go away?"

"Depending on how much you have ingested, it could take some time. Nevertheless, I have seen a few of my patients improve their health significantly once the source has been identified and eliminated."

"Then I will eliminate it," I replied. A mixture of fear and determination flushed through my veins. From this point onward, I would refuse any tea or bits of food presented to me by Melanie.

Thirteen

Unspoken Secrets

Upon my return, I felt as numb as the day I saw John and Melanie embrace. Needless to say, my disappointment about not being pregnant weighed heavily on my already broken heart. I wanted and needed a baby for both of our sakes. It appeared my prayers would continue to go unanswered. To make it even more depressing, now I knew it might be a challenge getting pregnant.

Beyond dealing with the fright of that revelation, I had been faced with the terrible possibility I had somehow ingested arsenic. Whether by nature or by the hand of a human, I was not sure. Nevertheless, I had deep-seated suspicions my tea contained more than the brew I loved to drink each morning.

I met Charlene in the parlor and could barely focus my mind. The white lines in my nails mesmerized me into a state of despondency. It did not take long for my host to inquire about my odd behavior.

"Did you have a pleasant tea this afternoon with your friend?"

I lifted my head at the sound of Charlene's voice. "Tea?" I replied, looking at her as if I hadn't an inkling of what she was talking about. Thankfully, my memory prompted me about my earlier lie. "Oh, tea," I exclaimed. "Yes, it was. . . "

My voice trailed off into silence as an overwhelming bout of tension swept over me, stealing the breath from my lungs. Tears streamed down my cheeks, and I sobbed loudly like a baby in front of John's cousin, who I barely knew. She reached out and touched my hand.

"Good gracious, Ann, what is wrong?"

"Oh, Charlene, I have no one to talk to, and so much is weighing on my heart." My short confession did nothing to allay my apprehension.

"If it makes you feel better, I do have a good ear for listening," Charlene replied. "Even though we are barely acquainted, I hate to see anyone in such a state of misery."

After sniffing a few times and wiping my face with the palm of my hands, I looked into her eyes. Her soft voice and sincere words encouraged me to bear my heart.

"I didn't have tea with a friend," I began. "I lied to you."

"You must have reasons," Charlene replied with little alarm.

"I went to see a physician hoping to find out if I might be pregnant."

"And are you?" she asked enthusiastically, reaching out and squeezing my hand.

Words failed me, so I merely shook my head no.

"Oh, I'm so very sorry," Charlene said. "John will be disappointed no doubt."

"It's more than that," I added. My voice trembled while I considered telling her everything.

"More than what?" she asked.

"It appears I am ill due to arsenic poisoning of some sort either from the water or elsewhere."

"Elsewhere?" Charlene squawked. "What do you mean elsewhere?" Her eyes widened in horror. "Certainly, you are not accusing John of doing anything so dreadful to you."

"No, but there is another who may wish to do me harm because of John," I replied. My eyes warily waited for Charlene's reaction.

"Melanie," she said with acute certainty. Charlene lowered her eyes and shook her head.

"I'm aware of their affair," I swiftly answered to dispel any conjecturing on her part of what knowledge I possessed.

"You know?"

"Yes, I know. Tell me how long this has been going on and why?"

"A few years before you wed," she admitted.

"Why on earth did he become involved with a chambermaid?" Even saying it sounded repugnant to me. "Is it love or lust?"

"A combination of both, I believe. John has not discussed with me his emotions in the matter."

"Well, how did you find out?" I pressed her for more information as to why she, above everyone else, was privy to the scandalous secret.

"Because he knew of my affair with a young man that my parents did not approve of, and I supposed he wanted to counsel me by example."

"Counsel you?" I thought her explanation to be odd.

"Well, if he loved her so much why didn't he marry her instead of me? I would have been spared this shame instead of having to endure it day in and day out." My high-pitched voice rose.

"Because John did not wish to disappoint his parents," she said. Her words confirmed my reasoning all along—duty to his family and title.

"Obligation to his father but no loyalty to me," I replied sadly.

"There is more than you know," Charlene added. "His heart has been torn over this matter for some time. There are fond emotions he carries for you, even though he may not feel at liberty to express them."

"He commits adultery behind my back, and you say he has fond emotions?" I whimpered about to cry again. "Love does not act in such a manner."

"Go home, Ann, and speak with your husband. There is nothing more that I can share with you regarding their affair," she somberly stated. "It is not my place to involve myself in private matters of the heart, especially where it concerns John."

Charlene's demeanor quickly changed, which I found most disheartening. A door had been slammed in my face, barring me from seeing the truth.

"Why won't you speak of it?" I vehemently complained. "She might very well be trying to kill me to get him back."

To my utter surprise, Charlene stood to her feet. "You should return to Blythe Court as soon as possible," she advised sternly. "I reiterate that I will not tell you what knowledge I possess about John's affair."

Charlene abruptly departed and left me alone in the parlor to stew in anger over her dismissal of my inquiries. I could not stay another hour in her household, knowing some secret remained undiscovered back home.

After packing my bags, I asked to be taken to the train station. I boarded the last train to Dorchester, scheduled to arrive at ten o'clock in the evening. Afraid of what I might find upon my return, I braced myself for the worst possible scenario.

The three-hour train trip helped to calm my nerves and gather my thoughts. I feared to find Melanie in John's room. I hoped that he had more sense than to display infidelity openly, which could be discovered by others on the staff. Of course, I still wondered how ignorant they were of the affair that had been ongoing for some time.

When my hired carriage arrived back at Blythe Court, I hoped to slip upstairs to my room and explain the reason for my early return tomorrow. Unbeknownst to me when I arrived at the front entrance, another carriage waited in the drive. I saw the crest on the door and immediately recognized the duke's coat of arms. I found it odd that his parents had decided to visit Blythe Court when he and the duchess had not done so since the day we wed.

I cautiously entered the hall and heard the voices of John and his father in the drawing room. Mr. Rhodes greeted me. After he had taken one look at my distressed countenance, his brow furrowed in concern.

"My lady, you are back already? Is everything all right?"

"Yes, fine," I answered, not wishing to look at him in the eye lest I struggle with tears. "I see his grace is here. You need not announce my arrival. I'll retreat to my room and talk to my husband later." As I turned to run up the stairs, John must have heard our voices and called after me.

"Ann!" he anxiously yelled as he approached. "I thought you were spending the night in London."

"Change of plans," I said, looking mortified. His father walked out from the sitting room and joined the conversation.

"You needn't run off, Ann," the duke said. "Come join us."

My eyes darted back and forth between my husband and his father. "I wasn't feeling well, so I came home early. Please forgive me for declining your offer."

"Is there anything I can do?" John asked, taking a step toward me with alarm on his face.

I shook my head negatively. "No. I need a good night's sleep, that is all. If you would be so kind as to excuse me, I would like to retire."

"Yes, of course," he answered.

"Goodnight, your grace." I nodded to his

father and slowly walked up the stairs to emphasize my fatigued condition. Mr. Rhodes followed me carrying my suitcase.

"Is there anything else you might need, your ladyship? Shall I fetch Melanie to tend you?"

"No," I sharply replied. She was the last person on earth I wanted to see. Even the sound of her name brought physical unease.

"Very well."

Mr. Rhodes exited my room and shut the door behind him. I closed my eyes and heaved a deep sigh. My nerves were frayed to such an extent that my hands trembled. I did not care to tend to my clothes, so I merely undressed and readied myself for bed.

After climbing under my blanket, exhaustion burdened my body. It had been a terribly long day traveling six hours back and forth, plus my examination and stressful conversation with Charlene. I did not wish to speak to anyone. The only goal I had in mind was to close my eyes and forget about my heartaches. Thankfully, John did not attempt to wake me from my slumber.

FOURTEEN

FINAL CONFRONTATION

My husband entered my bedchamber the following morning and sat on the edge of my bed. His arrival startled me. I rolled over and rubbed my eyes. His warm and comforting hand touched my shoulder, and he softly spoke.

"I'm worried about you," he said. "Are you feeling any better?"

I turned my head away, afraid that I would sob. My heart yearned to tell him I carried his child. Instead, I prepared to open another wound.

After heaving a deep sigh, I sat up in bed. My arms grabbed my pillow, which I clung to my chest tightly as if to shield myself from the hurt that would momentarily transpire.

"No, I am not better," I began, carefully choosing my next words. "John, I must dismiss Melanie as my lady's maid."

He scowled. "Dismiss? Why?"

"Because I believe she is trying to poison

me by placing arsenic in my morning tea." Of course, my sudden declaration sounded entirely irrational. He probably thought I had lost my mind.

"How preposterous," he quickly said, dismissing my allegation. "What proof do you have of such grave misconduct?" His eyes darkened.

"A physician's confirmation," I responded harshly. My body stiffened, preparing for battle as I drew my own sword to defend myself.

"What do you mean?"

His hand dropped from my shoulder and now tightly squeezed my upper arm demanding answers.

"I didn't go dress shopping yesterday. Instead, I went to a family physician in London because I have been ill of late with nausea and headaches. He examined me and seems to think I have been ingesting small portions of arsenic daily. Our water supply might be tainted, but I quickly dismissed his assumption since no one else in the household is sick."

For a brief moment, I glanced angrily at

his hand, clutching me. Seeing my disagreeable frown, he pulled away. Suddenly, he stood to his feet, posturing himself defensively.

"Why in the world would Melanie wish to poison you?"

Even though his statement sounded innocent, I had reached the end of my patience over the travesty of our relationship.

"Don't play your charade with me any longer, John. I know all about the two of you," I said. My voice trembled as I continued. "She is in love with you, that is why, and jealous of my position as your wife."

"What do you mean, *you know?*" His complexion paled, and his torso stiffened.

"After we returned from our honeymoon, I took a morning ride and saw you embrace and enter the cage together." I threw back the covers, got up from bed, and faced him. He took a step backward. "You played me the fool very well."

"You know nothing," he heatedly replied. John spun around and flopped in a nearby chair. He lowered his head into his hands and sat there quietly for a few moments, composing his emotions.

"Enlighten me, will you?"

John raised his head and looked at me with a forlorn gaze. He opened his mouth as if he were going to speak and quickly shut it again.

"Tell me, please," I begged him. "You owe me that much. I've known since the day I met you that something was not right." He continued to hide face. "Look at me, damn you!"

He inhaled a deep breath and expelled a long-drawn-out sigh. After a few moments of silence, he spoke. Slowly, he lifted his gaze and looked at me, his jaw tense with emotion.

"Three years before we wed, I had been an impetuous fool of a young man. I struggled with my father's overbearing demands, damned him behind his back, and set out to show him I would be my own person regardless of his edicts." His voice trembled, and he inhaled a shaky breath.

"So to make a statement on independence, you pursued a chambermaid?" I asked, shaking my head over his youthful folly.

John appeared to strengthen as he continued his explanation. Slowly standing up, he stood in front of me and continued.

"Melanie caught my eye with slight flirtations, which I eventually took advantage of when no one noticed. I found her to be delightful and susceptible to my attention and affection." He halted momentarily and then furrowed his brow. "Above all, Ann, she listened to me and my frustrations. She had seen, like the others on staff, my father's overbearing treatment being his only son and destined to take my place as a duke. I believed she understood my struggles when no one else cared."

"How convenient," I said disdainfully. Frankly, I couldn't comprehend his reasoning. It seemed weak and illogical, and I wondered if he were merely a scoundrel in character with no conscience. "So you began an affair?"

John hesitated, drawing in a quick breath but then relented. "Yes, we started an intimate relationship that continued for some time."

"Did you love her? Tell me the truth," I pressed with gritted teeth.

"I believed so at the time."

"Oh, my God, John," I moaned. A lump formed in my throat from the painful, long-overdue confession by my husband. The first slice of his sword inflicted a deep wound, I sat back down on the edge of the bed, dizzy and faint.

"Apparently you still do," I replied with certainty of voice. "I fully understand now why you treat me so coldly."

"No, you are wrong, Ann. When I knew we were to wed, I told Melanie I did not wish to keep her as my mistress. I haven't visited her bed since we married. I swear it."

"Liar," I shot back at him. "I saw you with my own eyes, embrace her, and lead her into the cage alone."

"You saw nothing," he adamantly replied. "There are reasons we met, which I cannot reveal to you."

"What reasons?" I shot back in anger.

"I cannot say."

Another door to the truth had shut in my face. "Well, then, Melanie still loves and wants you, otherwise why would she try to harm me?"

John sat back down in the chair, dangling his arms over the rests. Obviously, he could not comprehend that Melanie wished me harm. As he sat staring at the floor before him, I inquired further.

"Did she offer to stay with you as your

mistress?"

"Yes, but I refused because she deserves much better," he replied.

"Then it makes all the more sense to me that she should wish me harm since you did not set her up in a situation of provision and honor by being your kept woman." My face turned sour at the thought of it.

"I sincerely doubt she is responsible for what ails you," he shot back defiantly, continuing to defend her honor.

"Then you are blind if you think she is innocent," I snarled.

"At my request, she has kept her distance from me and not shown her affections outwardly. I know they still exist, but I no longer reciprocate them in any fashion."

"But you embraced her!" I ranted. "I saw the two of you with my own eyes."

"By greeting, only, not from love," he sternly asserted. "I know you find that hard to believe, Ann, but I no longer love her. My affections are for you as my wife."

"Affections," I laughed aloud. "What affections?"

"Ann. . ." he began in a reasoning voice.

"I want her gone from this household

today," I spat. "If you are telling me the truth, you will dismiss her immediately for both our sakes."

"I cannot," he replied, rising to his feet. "You may hire another lady's maid, but Melanie will stay on in another position as a chambermaid in our household if she so chooses. After all, you are the one who insisted Melanie be your attendant in the first place."

"Which might have been a good time to confess your relationship before I did, you scoundrel!"

My body trembled in anger. John's response incited me to such fury that I took a bold step forward and slapped John hard across his face. He showed no reaction but merely stood there looking at me as if he deserved my wrath.

"You have every right to be cross with me and filled with distrust," he somberly spoke. "All I ask is that you believe me when I tell you that we are no longer lovers, nor do I wish to be."

"Then dismiss her from Blythe Court," I reiterated.

He shook his head negatively. "My word stands. She will not leave Blythe Court."

The gruff tone of his voice and dark eyes told me I had no say in the matter whatsoever. He had taken the stance of ruling over his wife and property.

"I will tell her of your decision that you no longer want her services, and that she is to be reassigned," he offered. "Also, I will speak to Mrs. James to make sure she assigned to rooms of the estate where she will not be in your presence or mine."

"No, let me tell her so I may keep an ounce of dignity as your wife in this decision," I insisted.

"No," he loudly countered. "It must first come from me. Afterward, you can have your word with her, but I ask you to do so with civility."

"Civility?" I shut my eyelids and pursed my lips together at the notion of being polite to a woman who might be attempting to kill me. He asked too much of me.

"I promise you nothing," I countered in a huff. "If she is indeed responsible for my ill health, she deserves to receive the sharpness of my tongue if not more."

The thought of her staying at Blythe Court frightened me to the core. Even if she no longer served as my lady's maid, she would still have opportunities to harm me. Why did he demand that she stay? She had duped him into believing that she was a harmless servant, rather than a scorned woman who sought revenge.

"I am truly sorry for any pain this situation has caused you," he said broodingly. "If you remember, Ann, I warned you not to love me. Now, you know why. I've feared since the moment we met that this day would arrive, and its painful reality has harmed you."

Brokenhearted, I stared at him in disbelief. Yes, he warned me, but I chose to disregard his plea.

"I cannot prevent my heart from loving whom it will—whether it be a wise or unwise choice," I replied. "My only regret, John, is that you do not love me in return."

He looked at me with emptiness and lips that remained closed, and I knew a declaration of love would not be forthcoming.

"Go, then," I said, turning away from him and stifling my tears. "Tell Melanie that she is forbidden to serve me any longer."

"As you wish," he said, turning and heading for the door. He left, shut it behind him quietly, and I wept bitter tears at his departure.

While tending to my needs, I felt devastated. My confrontation with John had been far more difficult than I anticipated, leaving my heart shattered. I wanted to believe that he had ceased relations with Melanie since our wedding but could not bring myself to do so. How could I trust him after the heated embrace I witnessed exchanged at the tower?

Later in the morning, I searched for Mrs. James, the head housekeeper, and inquired if she could recommend someone on the staff capable of taking over Melanie's duties. I discovered that John already discussed the matter, and she informed me everything had been settled. A seasoned chambermaid interested in the advancement would be introduced to me for my consideration. Melanie would take over her duties instead.

Regardless of who it would be, I decided to forgo morning tea in bed as long as my competition remained in the household. I became fearful, worried my new lady's maid might do Melanie's bidding by tainting my brew. Making cautious decisions would keep me safe, or so I hoped, from a jealous woman. I had no idea how long it would take to remove the poison from my system. Nausea and headaches persisted but were undoubtedly exacerbated from the overwhelming obstacles that I faced.

John disappeared for hours. I concluded he did not wish to see me due to his infidelities or embarrassment over the matter. My mind incessantly thought about his illicit affair. The ruminations only fueled my jealousy that she, in spite of her station in life, had been able to win his love. Melanie's sweetness and ability to listen to him had drawn John to her. It appeared that I had not reached that stage in our marriage. John continued to be an unsolved puzzle.

Fifteen

Invitation to Death

Before dinner, John met me in the parlor where he closed the door so we would not be disturbed. I knew what the discussion would entail but had not expected to see such a pained expression on my husband's face. His reddened eyes accented his pallid countenance as if he had recently shed tears.

"Sit with me," he said. John stretched out his hand, palm up, and waited for me to take it.

"All right." When I touched his fingers, they were ice cold. He directed me to the settee, and we sat down together. John continued to hold my hand. I did not attempt to pull it away, thankful for the closeness even during this tense moment.

"After our discussion this morning, I summoned Melanie into the parlor and spoke to her in private."

"It must have been difficult for you," I

replied. Clearly, it had been a challenging task by the tense look on John's face.

"Unfortunately, it did not end pleasantly," he began. "When I told her that you did not wish her to serve you any longer because you discovered our past together, she flew into an inconsolable rage."

"Rage?" I had pictured her crying and pleading with John upon receiving the news, but not ranting and raving.

"I questioned her about the arsenic, and she vehemently denied her involvement."

"And you trust her," I said as if I already knew the answer.

"I'm sorry, Ann, but I still cannot conceive in my mind that she would do such a ghastly thing as to try to kill you." He paused for a moment. "If she had conceived anything so horrific, she should punish me instead as retribution for leaving our relationship."

"Well, I don't trust her," I admitted. "I shall always fear for my life as long as she remains in this house."

"You have nothing to fear from Melanie," he reiterated.

Each time he denied her involvement, I paused, searching his eyes for the truth. A part of me feared that he lied to protect Melanie. Why couldn't I trust his sincerity? I needed to ask him a question to test his motives.

"If she succeeded in murdering me and you thought it natural causes that led to my demise, would you have eventually taken her as your wife?"

John pulled his hand away and scowled me. "How can you ask me such an unspeakable question?" he indignantly challenged me.

Evidently, I wounded him in doing so, but he had not given me a response. "Well, would you?"

John stood hastily to his feet and looked down at me. "It's apparent to me that you have already answered that question yourself. Therefore, I shall not give you the satisfaction of responding either way."

A second later, he stormed from the parlor and left me alone. Another stabbing pain sliced through my abdomen. It had only been a day since I received no tea from Melanie's hand, but the symptoms persisted. Besides, I grappled with fatigue and weakness in my arms and legs. My emotional and physical wellbeing brought me to the brink of collapse.

Now that I expertly alienated my husband for asking what I thought to be a logical question, I refused dinner and returned to my room. I did not wish to speak about the situation any longer and instead sought sleep to rest and forget.

Morning arrived after spending the night alone. John did not return to speak with me after he stormed off from the parlor. While stirring in bed, a knock came at the door.

"Who is it?" I sat up and pulled the covers to my bosom.

"Mrs. James, your ladyship. I am here to introduce you to your new lady's maid."

After sighing in relief, I ran my fingers through my hair to try to straighten the unruly mess of curls. "You may enter," I answered.

The door opened, and Mrs. James arrived with another woman who I had seen occasionally. She wore the same black dress with a white collar and cuffs as Melanie. Rather than being young, she looked to be in her forties.

"Your ladyship, this is Margaret MacDonald. She would like to serve you for the next few days as your attendant. If you approve of her skills, she desires to remain in the position."

"Very well," I said.

"Your ladyship," Margaret said, curtsying. "It's a pleasure to serve." Her thick Scottish accent brought a smile to my face.

I watched as she carried the tray of hot tea and bread to my night table. Dread washed over me, and I glanced away as if I were looking at death itself.

"Mrs. James, I know it's the custom to bring me tea and bread in the morning, but I think that I would like to dispense with the practice immediately."

"Why is that, your ladyship?" She cocked her head at me apparently surprised over my break in protocol.

Why. My mind spun around in circles trying to come up with an answer to spurn the morning household ceremony. "It spoils my appetite for breakfast, frankly." My excuse sounded reasonable. "I would rather wait to partake of my morning tea and toast in the dining room."

"As you wish, my lady," she replied, readily accepting my explanation. She turned toward Margaret. "Well, I shall leave the two of you alone to get acquainted."

Mrs. James retreated and closed the door behind her. I cautiously lifted my eyes to my new lady's maid, leery of her presence. My paranoia increased another notch.

"Is it your habit to bathe in the morning?" she asked, smiling at me kindly.

"About four or five times a week," I answered. "I know it's excessive, but I enjoy a hot bath."

"Would you like me to fetch a chambermaid to bring water this morning?"

Chambermaid. Even the title brought fear. "As long as it's not Melanie," I replied, pulling my eyes away not wishing to see her reaction.

"Of course, your ladyship." She picked up the tray. "I will return your tea to the kitchen and summon water for you." Before doing so, she slipped her hand into her pocket and retrieved an envelope. "Please forgive me, but I've been asked to give this to you by Miss Wright."

Her trembling hand held out an envelope, and I stared at it in suspicion. Naturally, I hesitated taking it, but my curiosity incited me to do so.

"Thank you," I said, snatching it with my fingers. Margaret looked relieved that I had taken it and not reprimanded her for offering to deliver the note. "You may go now."

"Thank you, your ladyship."

After she had departed, I stared at the envelope for some time before finding the courage to open and read the contents. What could she possibly want? Maybe it was an apology and a plea for forgiveness so that she could win John's favor. I had given her more credit than I cared to extend.

Cautiously, I slipped out the paper from the envelope.

Marchioness,

His lordship has expressed to me your wishes. You had every right to dismiss me from my position. However, I know that you possess lingering questions about my relationship with your husband.

If you would be so kind as to meet me this afternoon, I will reveal everything to you to put this matter to rest. Perhaps it will bring peace to us all.

I will be at the cage at two o'clock and hope to see you there so that we may speak in private.

    Your humble servant,
    Melanie

Her words sounded to some extent repentant, but could I believe them? I did have lingering questions about their relationship that needed to be answered. Due to John's unwillingness to pursue the subject further with me, I suspected that I would never know the entire truth unless I sought it myself.

I placed the opened letter on my night table. At two o'clock, I would excuse myself for the meeting to discover if their relationship had ended. If it had, I wanted her assurance that she accepted things as they were. Otherwise, I would have no peace while living at Blythe Court with Melanie in our household.

Sixteen

Tragedy & Truth

Lured to the cage by Melanie, I arrived at two o'clock, anxious for honest answers. A few hours beforehand, I connived that I might convince her to leave if she would accept financial help. Surely, John would agree to such an arrangement for the sake of our marriage. I could not find any reason for him to keep her at Blythe Court except for his own pleasure.

As I pushed the door open and entered the interior, the same dim lighting filtered through the cracks of the shutters. I expected to see Melanie come out from the shadows to greet me, but the room was silent.

"Melanie?" I called her name and glanced around the first floor. She was not there, so I climbed the stairs to the second story. "Melanie?" My first reaction was to check the bedchamber, but I found it empty.

After glancing up to the staircase, I noted

that the door to the roof had been left open. Thinking that she had retreated outside for a breath of fresh air, I climbed another flight of stairs. As soon as I exited out-of-doors, I was blinded by the bright sunlight. I squinted, shielded my eyes with my hand over my brow, and glanced about the area. Melanie stood on the far side of the roof looking out over the landscape, not far from where John and I once stood together when we first met.

"Melanie?" I called after her as I approached.

Upon hearing my voice, she slowly turned and looked at me. At first, she appeared void of emotion, but I detected a glint of disdain in her eyes as I drew near.

"Here we are," Melanie began, taking a few steps in my direction. "Two women in love with the same man."

The sarcastic tone of her voice terrified me. I realized the conversation would not be a pleasant one. "Yes, but only one woman is married to him," I quickly clarified. Melanie flashed a smug grin.

"And if it weren't for you," she said, sounding like a hissing cat, "John would still be visiting my bed instead of sharing yours."

Melanie's tone, laced with malice, indicated she had no intention of making amends. I swiftly changed my attitude and verbally accosted her to get to the truth.

"Is that why you poisoned my morning tea with arsenic?"

"How did you discover my little game? I thought it quite amusing actually," she said void of any remorse.

"My physician recognized the symptoms," I said. "I would have dismissed you immediately, but it appears you still have a few of your claws in John that have not yet been released."

"If I wanted to kill you right away, I would have poured in a lethal dose," she blatantly admitted. Melanie took an aggressive step toward me, and her eyes darkened. "However, I found more pleasure in adding only enough to make you miserable with stomach pain and headaches before I did away with you completely."

Melanie's confirmation only solidified my intent in ridding myself of her. "One way or another, I'll see you out of Blythe Court for good," I seethed through clenched teeth.

"You are quite right in your assumption,

my lady," she replied, eyeing me with loathing. "One of us will leave, but death will be the doorway by which this entire affair ends."

All of a sudden, Melanie reached out and grabbed my hair with both of her hands and began yanking me forward. She confronted me with such ferocity that I screamed from the pain in my scalp, horrified that she would rip every strand from my head. The agony was so great that I became helpless. If I pulled away, she tugged harder, so I let her drag me forward to relieve the terrible pain.

"Let go of me!" I screamed at the top of my voice, hoping someone would hear me. My arms flailed wildly trying to hit her but failed.

She released her grip but wrapped her arm around my waist, dragging me toward the edge of the roof. Already weak from the poison in my body, I did not possess the strength to wrestle myself away from her death grip even though I desperately tried.

"In a minute, you'll be flying to your eternal rest," she growled.

When we reached the edge, she pushed me against the waist-high stone edge and attempted to shove me over. I fought and screamed, but what little power I possessed evaporated as I tried to defend myself. She saw me falter and increased her efforts to give me one more shove to cast me down to my demise. Ready to die at her hands, I suddenly heard a screeching voice.

"Melanie, don't!" John shrieked in panic.

Melanie spun me around and wrapped her arm around my neck so tight I thought she would snap it like a twig. He cautiously came within a few feet of us and halted.

"Let her go, Melanie, please," his trembling voice pleaded. John's eyes radiated horror. "Killing her will solve nothing."

"It will solve everything," she replied, heaving between breaths. "I find it impossible to share you with her any longer. My heart cannot bear the pain of losing you so you will lose her instead."

"You said you understood," John replied softly. "I thought you accepted our arrangement."

Arrangement? My mind whirled around in terror, trying to understand their cryptic conversation.

"Yes, at first. But after you wed, I realized

that I could not continue," she replied dispassionately. "As I saw your affections turn from me and grow for her, one of us had to go."

She tightened her grip around my neck, and I begged for mercy. "Melanie, please release me," I pleaded, gasping for breath.

"Release Ann," John anxiously beseeched. "We can talk about this rationally. If you kill her, you will have no future with me and will hang for your crime."

John reached his hand toward me, but he was too far away for me to grasp it.

"Please think what you are doing," he said. "This will only end in tragedy for all involved."

A few silent moments passed between us while my heart thumped wildly in my chest. Melanie reduced her grip as she considered John's warning. Her irrational actions had ruined whatever future she once held. If she killed me, she would die too. John would never recover from the loss.

"Please," I begged once more with hot tears streaming down my face. Her arm suddenly trembled. A second later, she released her grip, and I ran into John's arms for protection. He gathered me and wrapped me defensively in his embrace.

"Thank God," he said, clinging to me ardently.

My eyes shifted to Melanie, who looked at us with an empty stare of brokenness and defeat. A moment later, she glibly smiled as if she accepted the inevitable. A despairing look in her eyes inferred the unthinkable. Before I could say or do anything to dissuade her choice, to my utter horror, she flung herself over the edge. A second later, I heard the hard plop of her body hit the ground below.

"No!" John bellowed. He released me and ran forward, peering over the barrier of the rooftop. "Oh, dear God!"

My husband ran past me and down the stairs. I followed behind, shocked at the tragedy unfolding before us. When I arrived outdoors, John kneeled next to her lifeless body. Melanie lay limp in his arms as he repeatedly called her name. I brought my hand to my mouth as tears ran down my cheeks. The truth of their relationship unfolded in heartbreak. He had once loved her, and even after we wed, he cared for her wellbeing. A moment later, I fell to my knees, sobbing in empathy over his terrible grief and thankful to be alive.

John arranged for Melanie's burial at a nearby churchyard on the estate. Since the terrible affair, he had been estranged and distant. In wisdom, I kept my distance understanding his need to mourn.

When the time came for the funeral, he did not ask me to stand by his side. Distraught about the tragedy, I decided to watch from a distance. Practically the entire household staff stood around the coffin. John stared blankly at the hole where her body would be lowered to rest. If he hadn't discovered Melanie's letter laying open on my night table that terrible day, I would have been the one dead in a dark casket.

As I hid peering around the trunk of a tree, I could barely see the ceremony from where I stood. Mr. Rhodes and Mrs. James stood on each side of him as if they were pillars of strength. Surely, they must have known of his relationship with Melanie.

The vicar pronounced the last few words. I could not blame Melanie for loving him. We both suffered the pain of unrequited love in our relationship with John. Though she took her life, I prayed for God's mercy.

Each person quietly left the graveside, but John remained behind gazing at the coffin. My heart broke for him, so I came out from hiding and drew near to his side. He ceased his forlorn gaze upon my arrival.

"I'm sorry for your loss, John. Truly I am." My voice quavered with my own emotions. To my surprise, he put his arms around me and embraced me tightly. We stood together for what seemed like an eternity, and I lost myself in the beat of his heart against my ears.

"I have something to show you," he said. "No more secrets."

He pulled away, took my hand, and walked me toward the carriage. After giving directions to the driver, I climbed inside and sat next to him, wondering where we were going. Aware of his raw emotions, I said nothing and quietly held his hand.

The carriage drove into Dorchester and stopped at a line of row houses. "Why are we here?" I glanced about trying to find the reason for coming to this part of the city.

"You will soon find out," he said. He took

my hand and led me to the door. After knocking softly, a woman opened it and immediately curtsied upon seeing John.

"Your lordship," she said.

"This is my wife, Ann," he announced. "Ann, this is Melanie's aunt, Jane Wright." Confused by the introduction, I questioned why we had come to visit and surmised it might be to speak of the funeral and give our condolences.

"Pleasure to meet you. Won't you please come in?" she said.

As I entered into the modest household, she looked at me curiously.

"We've laid your niece to rest," John announced. "I'm sorry for your loss. Truly, I am."

"Thank you, your lordship, for taking care of the arrangements. It is much appreciated."

I wondered why her aunt didn't attend the funeral, and my question was answered when I glanced down the hall and witnessed a child running toward us. Her curly, long dark hair bounced up and down with each stride, and a bright smile spread across her face as she headed straight for my husband. A moment later, John kneeled down and scooped her up in his arms. He kissed her tenderly on the cheek, and she curled her arms around his neck.

"How's my little girl today?" he asked, giving her another smooch.

The darling child looked to be about two years old, and her face held the likeness of her father and mother. As the revelation unfolded before me, I suddenly saw all the pieces of the puzzle fall into place. John and Melanie had a child together. No wonder their bond had been so close. I should have been shocked and angry, but for some reason, I felt no negativity over the revelation. The child's blue eyes mesmerized me, bringing forth forgiveness from my heart.

"This is my daughter, Abagail," John said, turning toward me. "Now you know why her mother's affections toward me were so strong."

How utterly wrong I had been about everything. "And now I understand why your heart broke over her death," I replied sadly aware of the pain. "You had a child together."

"When Melanie told me that she would bear my child, I told my father of the affair. He made it very clear that I could not acknowledge the baby as my own. Instead, we arranged for Melanie to leave Blythe Court and live with her aunt during confinement. After the birth, she returned to our employ, but the child remained here with Jane." With fondness in his eyes, he continued. "Jane has been kind to raise Abagail for us."

"Is your mother aware, too?"

"Only my father," he admitted. "He is an expert at concealing family scandals. I swore to keep the secret upon his threats of disinheritance."

My poor father would probably have a heart attack once he learned his daughter married a man with an illegitimate child. Frankly, I found it quite humorous after all of his efforts to find me the perfect match. The duke did an excellent job of deceiving everyone, including me.

"Oh, John, why didn't you tell me?" I reached out, touched the child's cheek, and ran my fingers across her youthful skin. Her wide eyes looked at me, and she smiled. My heart melted into a puddle at my feet. She was so beautiful.

"How could I tell you?" he replied. "You would have never married me, and neither would your parents approve of the situation. The guilt I carried since the day we wed ate at my soul each time we were together." His hand reached out and pushed back a strand of unruly hair from his daughter's face. "The day that you saw me at the cage with Melanie, I had brought Abagail to visit her. Jane waited inside for her arrival, and the three of us visited together."

My eyelids closed. I wasted so many days believing a lie because of what I thought I beheld. If only I had known, perhaps Melanie would have reconciled with my place alongside John. I would have given her the acceptance and understanding she needed. Maybe she would not have viewed me as her enemy and ultimately given up life because of it.

"Can I hold her?"

"Are you sure?" He cocked his head, surprised about my request.

"Yes, please," I begged.

My arms reached forward, and to my surprise, she reached out toward me. When I had her securely in my embrace, I could not help but smile at the precious life.

"Hello, Abagail," I said. My eyes examined

every inch of her beautiful face. I had wanted to give John a child and had failed. Now, I could give him another gift instead.

"Can we bring her back to live at Blythe Court?"

John's eyes widened in surprise. "Are you serious, Ann?"

"Yes, my love. There is no reason that we cannot raise her together. After all, you are her father. She needs to be with you." I glanced over at Melanie's aunt. "That is if you don't mind," I added.

"No, my lady. I would be happy to see her with her father."

"I don't understand," John replied in a trembling voice. "How can you accept my illegitimate child with such grace and pardon?"

I smiled at him warmly. Now that I knew the truth, I loved him even more. "I told you once before that I have much to offer if you would only open your heart and take it." My eyes searched his. For the first time since we married, I witnessed his resistance to my love fade.

"Ann," he said, drawing close to me. "I'm sorry for having treated you unkindly." He leaned in and kissed me on the cheek. "My loving regard for you has been restrained by fear of rejection because of the secret I held."

"For Melanie's sake," I replied, "let us bring her into our home and give this little girl the life she deserves." John's eyes watered as he gazed at me in astonishment.

"Your willingness to embrace Abagail is more than I deserve," he said. He encircled us with his arms and whispered in my ear. "You have given me a gift of love, and it is love that I give you in return."

My heart felt as if it would burst upon hearing his words. An unspeakable tragedy had brought us to this moment. I determined then to keep Melanie's memory alive in Abigail's heart so that she would not forget her mother.

"Let's return to Blythe Court," I said, overcome with emotion.

John smiled. "Can you gather her things, Mrs. Wright?"

"Yes, your lordship. I'm pleased to do so."

She scurried down the hallway. Abigail reached out for her father, and he took her in his arms again. John's pride-filled gaze toward his daughter warmed my heart, and I found it endearing how he incessantly kissed her cheeks.

Melanie's death had been a loss to both John and her daughter. There had been times that I treated her cruelly in my attempt to win John's heart. Even my distrust of John throughout our marriage weighed as a grievous offense upon my soul now that the truth had been exposed.

In retrospect, I had not won John's heart by being a conniving woman. I won it because I understood and accepted him, regardless of his mistakes in the past. In return, he gave his love to me willingly, and I received it with humble gratitude.

Epilogue

When I accepted the little girl into our household, I no idea the consequences that would come of that decision. John had an inkling of what would transpire.

As soon as the duke and duchess learned of Melanie's death and our retrieval of John's daughter, they immediately returned to Blythe Court to put matters in order. My parents were equally upset when I broke the news to them, and my father vehemently complained that the entire family had been deceived. He demanded that I return home, but I refused.

It wasn't unusual, of course, for mistresses to bear children to aristocracy. I often wondered if I had half brothers or sisters wandering around London now that I knew my father had also wandered from my mother's bed. Naturally, I even questioned whether the duke had hidden scandals of his own making somewhere.

Regardless of my deductions regarding

the outcome of their morality, neither parents agreed with our decision to live with Abigail as our daughter. Instead, hypocrisy ruled their tempers rather than empathy. As far as they were concerned, the scandal of the illegitimate baby sired by the Marquess of Dorchester had to be squelched at all costs.

The duke, as he had done in the past, returned to his threats of disinheriting John should he continue with the idea of raising her openly in the household. In honesty, John thought they were veiled threats since his father had no one else to carry on the duke-dom after his demise. The family peerage had to continue, and no one but John was in line to be the next Duke of Dorset. Like a game of cards, John called his bluff but did make a concession for the sake of peace.

"I understand the need to protect the family name from scandal," John admitted. "However, I refuse to dispose of my daughter as if she didn't exist."

"Now see here," the duke ranted with veins bulging from his neck.

"We have a proposal, your grace," I inter-jected. "Please allow John to continue." The duke's eyes widened at my bold intercession, and he bellowed in response.

"Do you mean to tell me, young lady, that you have no objection to this illegitimate child coming to live with you?"

Without hesitation, I responded. "No, your grace, I have no objection. I love John and intend to support him. This child is his blood, and as his wife, I wholeheartedly accept the little girl into our home." For a brief moment, I hesitated to speak further but hoped to change his mind. "After all, the child has lost her mother, and I wish to give her stability and comfort."

John turned and glanced at me, and I saw in his gaze what I had longed for since the day we met. He turned toward his father.

"I love Ann. She is a gracious, kind, and forgiving."

"Well, frankly, I don't understand such nonsense," the duke replied. "Do you intend to go ahead with this arrangement in spite of my objections?"

John stood firm in front of his father, refusing to cower at his threats. "I will keep Abigail in our household as my ward for the time being. If anyone asks, Ann and I will explain that as a charitable concession on our behalf, we are taking care of the child whose parents are recently deceased," he proposed.

The duke narrowed his eyes, pondering the suggestion. "I need your word on my dying grave, that you will not reveal this child is your daughter as long as I am alive."

"Agreed," John replied. "Rather than bring disrepute to your name, while you live, I shall not divulge the fact that she is my daughter or your granddaughter, for that matter."

I thought John bold to remind the duke that his blood ran in Abagail's veins too. For a brief moment, the look upon his face indicated the point had hit home.

My parents agreed with the situation as well, thinking it wise and serving to everyone. At least John and I could in our own private way, raise Abagail and shower upon her our love and provision.

As fate would have it, John's father suffered a massive stroke six months later. John, now the Duke of Dorset, could do as he pleased. His mother, the dowager duchess, came to reside with us, and we welcomed her into our home as long as she acknowledged Abagail openly as her granddaughter. She agreed, having been more softhearted about the matter than her husband. The ruse came to an end, and Abagail bore John's name as his flesh and blood.

Over the years, our relationship grew closer, but I remained childless for some time. If it hadn't been for Abagail in our lives, my barren womb would have discouraged me. The little girl was most delightful in every way imaginable, and she kept John and I quite enamored with her antics. She retained the likeness of her mother, but it did not hinder my love for her in any manner. Abagail had captured my heart as if she were my own flesh and blood.

Nevertheless, John never gave up hope that I would conceive. At my doctor's suggestion, we had entertained one another in bed, exploring various positions to encourage conception. The passionate lovemaking between us continued, and never once did I think of the English countryside with my husband's abilities to keep me satisfied. Eventually, I became pregnant and bore him a healthy son that we named William Jonathan Broadhurst, the new Marquess of Dorchester.

Our relationship grew into one of mutual love, for which I thanked the heavens above. I had beat the odds, if you will, of not ending up like other aristocratic wives who accepted less in their marriages. Love and fidelity could be the better path in matrimony, and something in my heart told me that John would keep his promise until death parted us. After all, my earlier premonitions had come true, so I did not doubt that this one would lead only to happiness.

After all that had transpired, I learned a valuable lesson. Love has the power to change everything. Often it requires sacrifice and patience, but in due course, it does conquer all.

About the Author

With Russian blood on my father's side and English on my mother's, I blame my ancestors for the lethal combination of my DNA that influences my stories. Tragedy and drama might be found between the pages, but I eventually give readers a happy ending.

I live in the beautiful, but rainy, Pacific Northwest. My hobby (more of an obsession) is researching my English ancestry and expanding my family tree. To keep the memory of my ancestors alive, I often use their names in my novels.

My usual genre is historical fiction with romantic elements and historical romance set in the Victorian and Edwardian eras. My books include:

- The Price of Innocence (Permanently Free) - Book One of the Legacy Series
- The Price of Deception - Book Two of the Legacy Series
- The Price of Love - Book Three of the Legacy Series
- The Price of Passion - Book Four of the Legacy Series

- The Legacy Series Box Set (Books 1-4)
- The Phantom of Valletta (Featured in The Sunday Times, Malta in 2010)
- Dark Persuasion (2012 Finalist in the USA Best Book Awards for Romance)
- A Portrait of Perfection (A Dark Gothic Tale of Love and Betrayal)
- A Christmas Oath (2015 Christmas Novelette)
- A Christmas Mission (2016 Christmas Novelette)
- Lady Isabella (Ladies of Disgrace)
- Lady Grace (Ladies of Disgrace)
- Lady Charlotte (Ladies of Disgrace)
- Toil Under the Sun

Romance With a Kiss of Suspense (formerly under the pen name of Nora Covington)

- Thorncroft Manor
- Whitefield Hall
- Blythe Court
- Morland Park (Coming Soon)
- Romance With a Kiss of Suspense Box Set

Contemporary Romance:

- Conflicting Hearts, by J.D. Burrows - Contemporary/Women's Fiction.

Sign up for my newsletter and author blog by visiting my official website at http://vickihopkins.com